BLUESTOCKING'S BEAU

Jonathan circled the table slowly, his tread measured as he stepped closer. Rhian's eyes widened as he took her arm and led her to the garden door . . .

Under the full moon, in the midst of the overgrown garden, Jonathan gazed at her, his heart in his eyes. Rhian's breath was shallow and rapid. She watched him carry her hand to his lips and kiss her fingertips. She closed her eyes, shuddering.

Jonathan stepped closer and lifted her chin, willing her to open those glorious green eyes again. His mouth came down on hers, touching her lips tenderly. When she swayed toward him, he caught her in his arms, his touch like fire on her skin.

Rhian tilted her head back, her gaze of amazement causing Jonathan to smile. He kissed her again, this time more urgently, and Rhian met his demand, her passion stirred in a manner so new, so wondrous, all indecision was swept away with each new kiss, each tantalizing caress.

His tongue teased her lips and penetrated her mouth as Rhian's eyes opened to saucers. But exhilaration chased away surprise, and she moaned, molding her body against his . . .

WATCH FOR THESE ZEBRA REGENCIES NEXT MONTH!

LADY STEPHANIE   (0-8217-5341-X, $4.50)
by Jeanne Savery
Lady Stephanie Morris has only one true love: the family estate she has
managed ever since her mother died. But then Lord Anthony Rider
arrives on her estate, claiming he has plans for both the land and the
woman. Stephanie soon realizes she's fallen in love with a man whose
sensual caresses will plunge her into a world of peril and intrigue . . .
a man as dangerous as he is irresistible.

BRIGHTON BEAUTY   (0-8217-5340-1, $4.50)
by Marilyn Clay
Chelsea Grant, pretty and poor, naively takes school friend Alayna
Marchmont's place and spends a month in the country. The devastating
man had sailed from Honduras to claim his promised bride, Miss
Marchmont. An affair of the heart may lead to disaster . . . unless a
resourceful Brighton beauty finds a way to stop a masquerade and keep
a lord's love.

LORD DIABLO'S DEMISE   (0-8217-5338-X, $4.50)
by Meg-Lynn Roberts
The sinfully handsome Lord Harry Glendower was a gambler and the
black sheep of his family. About to be forced into a marriage of con-
venience, the devilish fellow engineered his own demise, never having
dreamed that faking his death would lead him to the heavenly refuge
of spirited heiress Gwyn Morgan, the daughter of a physician.

A PERILOUS ATTRACTION   (0-8217-5339-8, $4.50)
by Dawn Aldridge Poore
Alissa Morgan is stunned when a frantic passenger thrusts her baby into
Alissa's arms and flees, having heard rumors that a notorious highwayman posed a threat to their coach. Handsome stranger Hugh Sebastian
secretly possesses the treasured necklace the highwayman seeks and
volunteers to pose as Alissa's husband to save her reputation. With a
lost baby and missing necklace in their care, the couple embarks on a
journey into peril—and passion.

*Available wherever paperbacks are sold, or order direct from the
Publisher. Send cover price plus 50¢ per copy for mailing and
handling to Penguin USA, P.O. Box 999, c/o Dept. 17109, Ber-
genfield, NJ 07621. Residents of New York and Tennessee must
include sales tax. DO NOT SEND CASH.*

The Bluestocking's Beau

Donna Bell

ZEBRA BOOKS
KENSINGTON PUBLISHING CORP.

ZEBRA BOOKS are published by

Kensington Publishing Corp.
850 Third Avenue
New York, NY 10022

First Printing: May, 1996

Printed in the United States of America
10 9 8 7 6 5 4 3 2 1

For my very special father-in-law,
L. M. (Peko) Bell

And in Memory of my beloved mother-in-law,
Lois (Mamo) Bell

Part One

The Quest

One

> "Like the dew on a rose
> My heart in repose
> My love grows and grows . . ."

A sprinkling of applause filled the silence, and the flushed young man who had been speaking bowed humbly. A tall, angular lady with a tittering laugh thanked the poet and announced the serving of refreshments.

"Finally," muttered Jonathan Stirling, unfolding his cramped legs and rising. "I tell you, Pockets, one more . . ."

"My lord, how good of you to attend my little *soiree* this evening," gushed their hostess, blocking Jonathan's way to the dining room.

"My pleasure, Mrs. Bingley," said the dark-haired gentleman automatically. The starkness of his carefully arranged cravat and his black evening clothes were as uncompromising as his demeanor. His companion, smiling at him behind Mrs. Bingley's back, was his opposite— tall and casually dressed with silver-blond hair and an easy grace.

Their statuesque hostess bent her head to Lord Pembroke's and said with a smirk, "Of course, I know I have our dear Mr. Sims to thank for your presence. He, of course, is always to be found at our little literary gatherings. He is, of course, quite a favorite with us."

"Of course," echoed Jonathan, causing his friend to choke. Their hostess floated away, and Jonathan continued severely, "Why the deuce I allowed you to talk me into coming tonight, Pockets, I'll never know. How on earth you stand listening to all this drivel . . ."

"I would remind you, Jonathan, that my own work is sometimes numbered amongst this drivel," said the lanky blond man.

The viscount grinned at his friend and picked up a glass of champagne. He took a sip and frowned. "Even the champagne is watered," he muttered before returning to the topic at hand. "The difference, my dear Pockets, is that some of your poetry is actually decent."

Clive Sims—Pockets, to his friends—chuckled and pulled a notebook out of one of the four pockets on his unusual coat. "Must write that down on my schedule. April 2, Pembroke complimented my poetry."

"Some of it," corrected his friend, pointing at the page. "What is almost as bad, added to the wasted breath being spent on so-called literature, is having one's eyes assaulted by the most offensive collection of ill-dressed personalities ever gathered in one location. Belcher neckerchiefs in every hue, coats so loose they look like they are wearing their fathers' hand-me-downs, and the expressions on the faces! Mooning, mewling . . . puppies!"

Pockets's bark of laughter at this mixed metaphor rent the quiet gathering, but he recovered by turning it into a cough. Jonathan kindly slapped his back while continuing with his biting observations.

"And the females! It's no wonder you've managed to escape being leg-shackled! Positive antidotes! Oh, I beg

your pardon, madam," he said hastily, finding himself face
to face with one of the very antidotes.

"And yours, my lord," said the lady, the voice quietly
husky as she passed by, staring all the while at the floor.

Jonathan's eyes followed the sack-like, pea-green dress
for a moment, and he politely suppressed a shudder.

"She's probably very intelligent," said Pockets, his lips
twitching.

"Gad! What makes you think I would be interested in
an intelligent female?"

"Too much of a challenge?" asked Pockets.

"Hmph! Too much of a harridan!"

"You are a hypocrite, Jonathan. First you complain
about the lack of intelligence here; then you disdain an
intelligent lady."

"Sorry, Pockets, let's get out of here!"

"Not yet. There's an excerpt from a novel I want to
hear. Friend of mine, you know. I think you'll enjoy it."

"I doubt it," grumbled the viscount.

"Jonathan, I know we're not up to your intellectual
standards. I mean, I don't even pretend to understand
those Latin essays you're always translating."

"Greek, usually."

"Greek, Latin, Hebrew—makes no difference to me.
The point is, Jonathan, you've become an intellectual
snob. If it weren't for your other interests, you'd be a positive dullard. It won't hurt you to listen to a bit of poetry
or prose. May even widen your horizons."

Jonathan, who had followed his friend's scold with a
half-smile on his dark face, nodded. "Very well, I'll stay.
You have a point; but I warn you, the next selection better
be an improvement over the last, or I'm leaving."

"Agreed!"

The two men turned to listen, standing behind the rest of the seated audience. Pockets leaned forward slightly, his pale brow damp with perspiration and his blue eyes sparkling.

The young man in front smiled and began. His voice was deep and pleasant and carried easily throughout the room.

"I have been asked by a friend," here he paused as people nodded knowingly to their neighbors, "to read an excerpt from his novel entitled, *The Dastardly Duke*."

"The dastardly duke broke free of his bonds with a mighty pull. Leering, he leapt toward Lady Lovelace who fought feebly and futilely. Then the swaggering duke swept her into his arms; and she swooned. Cursing, the duke . . ."

Jonathan's mind wandered away from the dark forests and the dastardly duke. He made a mental list of his activities for the next day, promising himself to go to Manton's gallery for shooting as well as Tattersall's to look for another horse.

Suddenly, the dark hairs on the back of his neck prickled, just as they had on the Peninsula when he sensed danger. Jonathan turned slightly in his chair to find the occupant of the pea-green gown studying him. An arch of one brow sent her eyes elsewhere; this time he did not suppress the shudder. She appeared much too intelligent to him behind those thick spectacles she now sported—a veritable dragon of a bluestocking.

Finally, he forced his attention back to the gathering, listening in disgust to the conclusion which left Lady

Lovelace in chains in a rat-infested dungeon. The other guests began to applaud enthusiastically.

Shaking his head, Jonathan turned to his friend and said, "I don't know which is more pathetic, the fact that this author feels his work is good enough to be read in public, or the audience's lack of discrimination."

The silence descended like a guillotine. Jonathan looked past Pockets's reddening face to take in the sea of shocked, open-mouthed stares. Instantly, he knew the truth.

"Pockets, I . . ."

Clive Sims turned on his heel and Jonathan called, "Clive, wait!"

But Pockets was already at the door, calling for his hat and carriage.

With a nervous titter, Mrs. Bingley stepped in front of the viscount and said loudly, "Really, my lord, so naughty of you to tease Mr. Sims so! He thought you were serious!"

With a tremendous effort, Jonathan didn't throttle her. Instead, he took his cue and responded for all to hear, "I realized that too late, Mrs. Bingley. I shouldn't have teased him, but he must know I wasn't serious. Couldn't be! Demmed fine piece of work!"

The other guests nodded and began to chatter about the excellence of Mr. Sims's work. Jonathan thanked his hostess and bade her a hasty good evening before hurrying out the door.

The cool evening air hit his face, reviving him, clearing his head. He looked down the street to see Pockets's familiar coach turn the corner.

"Damn!" he muttered, plunging his hands into his pockets and starting down the steps.

Another coach, an old-fashioned barouche, pulled up and the door opened.

"May I drop you somewhere?" asked a husky feminine voice from the shadowy interior. By the dim light of the lamp, Jonathan recognized the homely female from the salon. He wouldn't dare comment on her looks, he thought; he had done enough damage with his mouth for one evening.

"Thank you," he said, climbing inside and sitting down by her side. "Allow me to introduce myself. I'm Jonathan Sterling."

His hard thigh touched Rhian's, and she hastened to move away, but her skirts were trapped.

"Pardon me," said Jonathan, moving to free the pea-green silk.

"Thank you, my lord," said Rhian breathlessly. Why on earth did she sound like such a peagoose?

"I appreciate your saving me a long walk, Miss . . ."

Rhian ignored his hint for her name and said, "Where can we drop you, my lord?"

"I'm staying with my friend, Clive Sims. Unless, of course, he's had my bags thrown into the street." He gave her a careless grin.

"I'm sure he wouldn't," said Rhian, wondering why she was suddenly tongue-tied. She had issued her forward invitation hoping to coax further caustic observations from the indiscreet gentleman. Instead, she was fighting a rising blush and finding it impossible to converse normally. It was not nerves—there were no butterflies fluttering in her stomach. Worse yet, she felt as if her blush was turning into a fever. She glanced up at her passenger.

He appeared completely at ease. Whatever she was feeling, it was not obvious to the handsome man at her side.

She expelled a tiny sigh of relief. It wouldn't do to draw attention to herself. In her guise as the mousy Lady Rhian, she strived for invisibility and achieved it indubitably.

"Where does Mr. Sims reside, my lord?" she asked.

"Number six, South Audley Street."

She relayed this news to her coachman but made no other conversation, keeping her head down so the lamplight shaded her face. Jonathan sat back on the seat, observing that the vehicle, though of excellent quality, was sadly in need of refurbishing.

"Do you often attend Mrs. Bingley's literary salons?" he inquired finally of the top of the woman's turbaned head.

She nodded again, but didn't speak. Intrigued, Jonathan said, "It was my first visit. I found it most, uh, interesting." He wasn't sure, but he thought he saw the corner of her mouth lift.

The carriage stopped and the door opened. Jonathan jumped to the ground. Looking back into the carriage, he said, "Thank you again, Miss, for saving me a long walk. My luck's been quite out all evening; I would probably have been set upon by footpads."

The woman lifted sparkling green eyes to his and a bewitching smile lit her face. "You're very welcome, my lord. It's been most enjoyable," said the husky voice. "Good-bye."

The door closed and the groom leapt up behind. As the carriage lumbered away, Jonathan recovered his senses. He took a step after the beauty before he realized it was futile

"Pockets!" he bellowed as he pushed past the surprised butler. "Pockets, I've just met the most extraordinary female!" he exclaimed as he entered the cluttered library and poured himself a Madeira. "And attending a literary salon, of all things!"

"How nice."

"Well, I wouldn't exactly call it nice. The devil of it is, I don't even know her name."

"Hmm."

"Beautiful eyes, though. Green, I think, but it was hard to tell in the carriage light. At first, I thought her an antidote. Then she looked up and—"

"So?"

"Pockets, don't you . . ." Jonathan looked at his friend's stiff countenance for the first time. "Oh, I forgot. You'd probably like to plant me a facer, wouldn't you?"

"Don't think I can't," said the tall, slender man, leaving his post by the fireplace to stalk back to the sideboard and pour himself another drink.

Jonathan smiled slightly. "I daresay you could, if you wished. But I hope you'll simply accept my apology. My comments were rash and inconsiderate—no matter if the author was my oldest friend."

"Apology accepted. I realize now I shouldn't have dragged you there," said the easy-going Pockets. He flopped down on the leather sofa and stretched his long legs toward the fire. "Was it really so bad?"

"I don't know. I readily admit I'm not very knowledgeable about modern, uh, literature. I suppose it was quite acceptable as far as that is concerned."

This pronouncement caused Mr. Sims's blue eyes to twinkle. "You, Jonathan, are a snob."

Rather than deny it, Jonathan raised his glass in a silent toast.

"So you think the novel was terrible?" pursued Pockets

like a small terrier worrying away at a stranger's pants leg.

"I thought it rather melodramatic," he began diplomatically. "But then, it would probably be a great success, Pockets, considering today's simple-minded readers."

"Now that's a backhanded compliment if there ever was one."

"But true, judging from the Minerva novels everyone reads so voraciously. They all claim to have read Miss Austen's works, but I can't believe it. The ton wouldn't recognize a decent piece of writing without the critics telling them how wonderful it is," snorted Jonathan, warming to his topic.

"So you are saying my work would be well received because it is so bad?"

Jonathan continued, heedless of his friend's rising ire. "What I am saying is our society has no idea what makes good literature. I wager I could write a novel that has every bit of melodrama and all the inane plot twists ever conceived, have it published, and get most of the ton to declare its magnificence merely by dropping a word here or there that everyone who is anyone has read the thing!"

"Done!"

Jonathan's mouth dropped open, and he glared at his friend. "You think to make a fool of me?"

Pockets chuckled and shook his head. "Not in the least. You said you would make a success out of a terrible novel so you could prove how little one should depend on the good taste of the Ton. Very well. Do so."

"I could do the same with someone else's novel," said Jonathan, beginning to regret his haste. Not that he couldn't produce a novel, especially a bad one. But it would take time away from his scholarly pursuits. And what if someone discovered him?

"I do believe you're afraid to try your hand at it, Jonathan," taunted Pockets, beginning to return his betting book to its pocket.

"Devil a bit."

"Then you'll do it?"

"Yes, I'll prove my point."

Pockets scribbled a few words before looking Jonathan in the eye and warning, "Mind you, you must make certain the thing is truly dreadful."

"What's wrong? Afraid I will turn out a better piece of literature than your Dastardly Duke?"

"Not a bit of it! Two thousand?"

"Done!" said the viscount.

Pockets replenished their glasses, and they drank to the new venture before settling back on the sofa in companionable silence.

Jonathan stared into the fire, the dancing light reminding him of the gleaming green eyes of his benefactress. Odd that he could still see her face—he, who rarely gave women a thought beyond how they might satisfy his own needs. But that Mona Lisa smile intrigued him, and those eyes ensnared his imagination.

"What was her name?" The question startled Jonathan; Pockets was a friend of unnatural perceptions.

"That's the damnable part. I haven't a clue. Obviously quality, but fallen on hard times. The coach was old, but well-cared for. Only the coachman and one footman in attendance. Never seen any of them before. Surely you've noticed her at the salons before."

After drinking deeply, Pockets shook his head and said,

"So, you have been bewitched by a lady whose name you don't even know. What color is her hair?"

"Couldn't say. She was wearing one of those Turkish things. But you saw her. It was the one in the ugly dress I almost ran into. Remember?"

"I remember seeing someone, but I don't know her. Perhaps Mrs. Bingley—"

"Never mind. If it means seeing the Bingley woman again, I don't think it's worth it."

"Even for such a beauty?"

"I don't relish the idea of having it bruited about that Viscount Pembroke is enamored of some anonymous bluestocking. Damn! Why didn't I insist she introduce herself?"

"Possibly because you thought her a 'positive antidote' and didn't really wish to further your acquaintance."

Jonathan grinned. "Quite right. It is my own fault. But never mind, there are many such beauties in London. One is about the same as another."

"My lady, I'm so glad you're home!"

With one hand Rhian pulled off the dreadful turban and with the other, she patted the frail shoulder of her butler in a familiar gesture. "What is it this time, Tippy?"

"M'lord has taken out the curricle with Rabelais in the traces."

Lady Rhian Ainsley stopped in her tracks, her lovely face a study of restrained panic. "By himself?"

"I sent Howard with him."

Speaking slowly, without a great deal of conviction, Rhian said, "Good. Hopefully, if they overturn, Howard will have enough sense to simply lead my horse home."

"I told him to, my lady."

"Then all we can do is wait."

"I'll have Mrs. Gilbert bring some hot chocolate to the library, my lady. And Fanny is waiting upstairs."

"Thank you, Tipton," said Rhian, starting up the stairs.

The old butler watched her go, her back ramrod stiff, her head up. "Pluck to the bone," he muttered.

It was bad enough when her father had lost his own horse in a game of faro, but this! And yet, faced with the news that her drunken parent had taken out his curricle with her only horse—on a damp, dark night—some ladies would have fainted; others would have ranted at their servants. But Lady Rhian was always reasonable, always fair. There was never so much as a raised voice; at least, not to the servants. The only person he had ever heard her raise her voice to was her sister—an understandable happening, knowing Lady Penelope, or Mrs. Banyon, as she now styled herself.

Half an hour later, Rhian heard the front door open, followed by a shout. She put down the book she had been reading and went to the library door.

"It's all right, my lady," gasped Tipton, helping the footman carry in her father who was shouting a bawdy song. "Henry's got your horse now."

Rhian looked down at her father who had grown silent and oblivious to the world.

"Unharmed?"

"Yes, m'lady, as close as I can tell," answered their footman/valet.

"The curricle?"

"None the worse for wear."

"Rabelais?"

"Threw a shoe, I think. Henry has him in hand, my lady."

Rhian nodded. "Thank you, Howard, for looking after my father. Would you see that he gets to bed?"

"Yes, m'lady."

Rhian watched dispassionately as the valet and butler struggled to get their heavy burden upstairs. She sighed, remembering days when. . . . But that was many years ago, and she had things to do.

Pulling a wooly shawl around her shoulders, she made her way to the back of the house, through the gardens to the mews. The two old carriage horses were dozing in their stalls, and she passed by to the next one where a light shone.

"Thrown a shoe, all right, 'enry, and bruised 'is foot, too, I'll be bound."

"Is it bad?"

The two servants stood up respectfully at the sound of her voice. The elder, a grizzled little man with powerful shoulders, said in a thick Scotch brogue, "Naught t' worry ye, m'lady. I kin set 'im t' rights."

"How long?"

"A week, mayhap a fortnight. Don't ye worry."

Rhian smiled and stroked the gray muzzle of her gelding. "Then I shan't worry. In the meantime, I'll take a hackney or the carriage. Just make sure his lordship doesn't forget and take him out for a ride."

"We'll try, m'lady. We'll try."

Rhian went back to the house and up to her room. She stirred the meager fire before slipping into bed and pulling the covers up under her chin. Only then did she allow

herself to relax and enjoy her thoughts of the handsome,
bitingly witty Lord Pembroke. Remembering his comments, she grinned; she threw back the covers and went
to her writing desk—a large, masculine affair, cluttered
with papers. She jotted down a few words and placed the
note on top of a stack of mismatched papers. With this
small task completed, she went to bed. Dreams of black
eyes enhanced her sleep, and when she awoke, it was with
a feeling of luxurious warmth.

Rhian sighed at her own foolishness and climbed out
of bed. She hadn't had such passionate dreams since the
age of sixteen when she had fallen head over heels for
the French dancing master at Mrs. Goodman's Seminary
for Young Ladies. But Rhian was a practical young woman
of twenty-four and wouldn't allow such dreams to disturb
her day-to-day routine.

An hour later, in the alley beyond the overgrown garden, she was climbing into the hackney cab she usually
engaged to carry her to the office. Only the glimpse of a
shapely ankle gave a clue as to her true identity. Certainly
the black, loose-fitting cloak and the bonnet with a heavy
veil gave nothing away.

After a short time, the carriage rolled to a stop outside
a large building in the city. It was not Fleet Street, but the
neighborhood was such that the driver kept one hand on
a large horse pistol. Rhian climbed down unassisted and
waved to the driver before entering the office building.

Though the outside of the structure matched the rest of
the neighborhood, the inside was another story. A neatly
attired clerk bade her a cheery good morning, and a maid
in a starched uniform curtseyed before returning to her
dusting. From behind a closed door there was the steady
clack of machinery.

Rhian bypassed this door and entered a large office, the centerpiece of which was a huge mahogany desk strewn with newspapers. It was a well-lighted room, the center of its ceiling being a glass roof.

She removed her bonnet and smoothed her fiery red hair. Next came the dowdy black cloak. The figure revealed by her simple, gray gown was tall and slim but rounded by curvaceous hips and firm breasts. Her complexion was a smooth peach with a hint of pink to the cheeks and lips. Hers was the type of beauty that years wouldn't dim, had there been anyone to notice.

Finally, Rhian sat down and began sorting through the stack of papers she had brought from home. The clerk knocked quietly and entered without waiting for her response.

"We've got a problem, Miss."

"Yes?"

"That Lady Filbert stormed in here insisting that we print a retraction about her and Mr. Cook in the next edition."

Rhian smiled and shook her head. "She hasn't a leg to stand on. I know what I said was true and so does half of London. But we aim to keep the peace, so a retraction it will be."

The young man smiled. "I daresay she'll not ask for another one. She'll realize soon enough that she shouldn't tangle with us."

"Now, Geoffrey, we don't want to be too harsh. A little 'the lady doth protest too much,' should suffice. You know what to say. I'll leave it to you."

"Thank you. Oh, one other thing. Your sister called yesterday afternoon."

"I hope she didn't harass you, too much," said Rhian with a grin.

"No, I just acted my usual meek self, and she left me alone. I think she'll be back though," said the young man, his eyes twinkling. "She can't have appreciated that review you did of her latest publication."

"You are the master of understatement, Geoffrey. Just show my sister in when she calls."

"Very good, Miss. Oh, Templeton says he's almost ready to print the next edition. Have you written the Quidnunc column yet?"

"No, but I have plenty of material. So much, in fact, I think we'll have to extend it. I wish you could have been at Mrs. Bingley's last night! You remember how dreadful I told you her 'literary events' have become. There was a new guest, Lord Pembroke, and he made the most wicked comments! I can't wait to print them!"

"The same Lord Pembroke the Patronesses of Almack's were threatening to ban?"

Rhian cocked her head to one side, remembering Lady Jersey's threats, and smiled. "It has to be. I'd forgotten about that."

"After today's issue reaches the drawing rooms, I doubt this Lord Pembroke will forget. Maybe you better save quoting last night's observations for a later date."

She appeared to be considering it, then shook her head. "He probably doesn't even know about the existence of our little newspaper. I'm not going to worry about him. Now, what else have we to do today?"

"Rhian, I have warned you before about your high-handed reviews, but this time it is the outside of enough!

Rubbish, indeed!" The matron planted in front of her desk possessed the same fine green eyes and fiery hair as Rhian, but here the resemblance ended. She was short and squat with an overly abundant bosom which, on this day, sported purple and white stripes that seemed to go on forever.

"Hello, Penelope," said Rhian mildly. "That will be all, Geoffrey. Tell Lizzie to bring in some tea, if you wi—"

"I don't want any tea! I wouldn't take tea with you if were you the last person on earth!" declared her sister, dropping heavily into the chair facing the desk. It groaned, but held.

"Sherry?" asked Rhian.

Her sister glared at her but nodded. Geoffrey hurried away. Rhian sat down and calmly smoothed her skirts.

"Now, what may I do for you, Penelope?"

"Do? Why, you may stop this vindictive criticism of the books I publish! I realize you are jealous that Grandfather chose to bequeath the publishing house to me, and only this little newspaper to you, but—"

"Not in the least, Penelope. I quite enjoy my little newspaper. And vindictive is a very harsh word, dear sister. Why would I need to be vindictive to you?"

Penelope sat up straighter and a gleam appeared in her eyes. "Perhaps it is because you are four and twenty, unmarried, childless, skinny as a walking cane, and bitter as a lemon."

Rhian smiled pleasantly. The words that at one time would have angered her missed their mark. "I prefer independent, slim, unfettered, and happy, but as you will. I won't bandy words with you over our very different lifestyles. You have chosen yours and I, mine."

"How long do you think the ton would invite you about

should they discover you not only own, but actually run this scandal sheet?" There was no mistaking the intended threat.

"Newspaper, if you please. And I dare say it would be about as long as they accepted you after you wed Banyon, the Irish banker." Rhian abandoned her comfortable posture and leaned forward, her eyes narrowing dangerously. "And as much as you might want to hurt me, I know you don't wish to alienate Papa. For though you disdain the ton, you still want your son to inherit the title." Penelope sniffed but remained silent, and Rhian continued more mildly. "With your fortune and the title, little William will be welcomed everywhere. Maybe he will even be able to turn that pile of an estate into something worthwhile."

The sisters exchanged a look of mutual understanding. Both had grown up with debt collectors at the door half the time and living in indulgent splendor the other half until their father's luck would change again. It had inspired in both his daughters a sense of frugality and determination. And it was the one thing that each sister admired about the other.

Lizzie brought in the tea tray, and Rhian poured Penelope a glass of sherry before fixing her cup of tea.

Seated again, she offered, "I could print a retraction."

Penelope held up both hands as though warding off an evil omen. "No! Thank you, but not this time!"

Rhian laughed softly and asked, "But what can I do?"

"Just . . . Oh, nevermind. I must be going. Good day. Do tell Papa I said hello."

"I will. Good-bye, Penelope."

* * *

"You have made the scandal sheets again, Jonathan," said Pockets to his breakfast companion.

"Indeed?" commented the darkly handsome recipient of this news, not bothering to look up from the Greek essay he was perusing. He made a note on a piece of paper beside his neglected plate.

"Says the patronesses of Almack's will deny you admittance when the Season begins this week if you persist in driving along respectable streets like a bat out of hell."

This evoked a rumble of laughter from Jonathan Stirling, Viscount Pembroke, who looked up at this and asked, "In those words?"

"No, it says, 'even Lady J has vowed revenge for the spots on her new gown.' " Clive Sims reached into one of the four pockets on the front of his brocade dressing gown and withdrew a small notebook. "That makes four of 'em. Two to go before the end of the week," he added thoughtfully. "Too bad you can't send 'em an invitation to come round together so you could finish all at once."

"Don't be ludicrous, Pockets. Where's the sport of that?" Jonathan stretched out his long legs under the gleaming table and leaned back thoughtfully. "I daresay they'll both be at that thing Lady Reynold is giving tomorrow. Might be able to get them both there. Course, I really hate the idea of spoiling the day for Lady Cowper. She's the best of the lot, you know."

There was no reply as Pockets chewed on the end of his pencil, his pale brow furrowed. He replaced his betting book and pulled out a second notebook from yet another pocket and began to scribble hurriedly. Jonathan stood up and left the room, picking up the newspaper his friend had forgotten and carrying it to his room.

He plopped down in the easy chair in front of the fire

and began to read the latest scandal sheet. In all fairness, he thought, it was better written than most and actually showed great wit. The London Report had been around for a number of years, but it had only recently become widely read by the ton—or so everyone claimed. Jonathan glanced over a review of the last novel of Jane Austen which everyone claimed to have read but which he suspected merely collected dust on many shelves. But "everyone" was talking about it. Jonathan, who had actually read *Northanger Abbey,* admitted it was good—for a novel. Being more of a scholar, he rarely took the time to read such works.

Then his glance fell to the social column where his name appeared. He smiled at the title of the column, "Quidnunc." So the editor was of a classical bent; not every man would know the Latin for gossipmonger.

The column itself contained the usual references to who was courting whom and whose entertainments were successful and why. But the quotations were precise and to the point. Obviously, the writer had been in attendance or had a very dependable reporter. Even the details of the bet he had made at White's when among friends were accurate. He had indeed vowed to "wash away the sins of" the patronesses of Almack's after they snubbed a friend's cousin by withdrawing her vouchers. It seemed the editor had the entree into the very best clubs and homes. And the biting sarcasm—he, too, had been witness to Lady Filbert's "fall from grace" with Mr. Cook when they had fallen out of their box at the opera with hands tucked into the most indelicate places on each other's persons.

Jonathan put the paper away and went to his desk, picking up a pen and repairing the quill before setting to work on translating the Greek essay he had been skimming at breakfast. During the next half an hour, he had recourse to his dictionary at least ten times. Searching his mind in vain for just the right word the eleventh time, he pushed back from the desk in disgust.

His restlessness was uncharacteristic. It was his custom to work each morning for two hours before going out. But he simply couldn't concentrate. There was no accounting for it, but it was so.

Jonathan finished dressing, his usual morning attire including a fitted coat by Weston, buckskin breeches and boots with a shine so bright he could see his reflection. He tied his cravat simply and brushed his thick, dark hair quickly before making his way down the stairs. His plans to go to Manton's shooting gallery were abandoned in favor of a visit to Tattersall's where he hoped to find a new riding horse for his niece.

He was immediately hailed by two acquaintances and he joined them at the ringside.

"Pembroke, I hear you're down to two victims and only three more days," said Lord Chuffington, making a note about the two-year-old being shown.

"Never fear, Chuffy, your bet is assured. I shan't let you down," said Jonathan.

"Never thought you would, old boy. Wouldn't have placed the wager else. Gambling, to me, is foolish. You know I only wager on sure bets. And you, my dear fellow, are a . . . sure . . . thin . . . What the devil are you staring at?"

Jonathan looked up quickly, saying, "Sorry, just admiring that emerald in your cravat."

"Oh, thank you. It was something I . . ."

Jonathan turned toward the ring to watch the paces of a six-year-old mare. His wandering mind had betrayed him again. But this time he knew the cause—something about that emerald had sparked his memory of those green eyes. They had bewitched him, he thought wryly, a smile forming on his lips.

"Like her, eh? Thought I might bid on her myself. I could use another hack."

Jonathan turned to his rotund friend and shook his head. "Not up to your weight, Chuffy. I saw a Belgian over there that—"

"All right, all right. No need for insults. I'll let you have her," said the good-natured Chuffy.

"Ah, if only that were in your power," murmured Jonathan, confounding his friend as he moved away from the crowd.

Two

Lord Pembroke was nothing if not disciplined. After he arose the next morning, he sat at his desk for two hours outlining a convoluted plot for his novel and trying several opening scenes.

At noon, Pockets knocked on the door and poked his head inside. He grinned as Jonathan turned his frowning visage toward the doorway.

"Not having trouble creating your masterpiece, are you?" asked Pockets, leaning against the doorjamb, his expression revealing how much he enjoyed such a prospect.

"Only in creating a bad one," snorted Jonathan.

"What? Are you saying there could possibly be a good novel?"

"Possibly," responded Jonathan. "But since I have agreed to write a bad one, it is rather difficult."

"Ha! I wonder, old boy, if it would perhaps have been better to wager that you couldn't write a good novel!"

"We'll never know, will we?" said Jonathan with a smugness he didn't feel.

Pockets came over to the desk, eyeing the pile of papers curiously. "How is it coming? Have you settled on a plot?"

"Not only a plot, but the main characters, the setting, everything. All here in my outline."

"May I?" asked Pockets, picking up the sheets of paper indicated. After perusing them, he said, "Doesn't sound too bad."

"Hmph! Sounds damned silly, and you know it."

"Well, you've got the evil lord of the manor, the poor but noble daughter of the vicar, and a dashing sea captain."

"Don't forget the dark and gloomy castle," said Jonathan dryly.

"Haunted, I hope," quipped Pockets.

"Goes without saying. And then there's the secret, tropical island with poisonous snakes and quicksand."

Pockets laughed. Then he frowned and said seriously, "you know, Jonathan, you're liable to write such an exciting novel, everyone really will like it, and I'll be out two thousand pounds."

"As improbable as this plot is, how can it help but be a success?"

Dressed in a pale gray gown, more elegant than the pea-green she had worn to Mrs. Bingley's literary salon, Rhian descended into the gardens at Lady Reynold's villa just outside London on the Thames. The sun was already in its zenith, and the al fresco breakfast was well underway.

Today, Rhian's red hair, covered by only a scrap of lace as befitted her spinster state, was scraped back into a neat chignon. No curls escaped to tantalize, and the neckline of her gown defied fashion and reached her collarbones. The thick spectacles she wore on the bridge of her nose were positioned so she could peer over the top. This gave her appearance a queer sort of questing quality and detracted mightily from her attractiveness, which suited Rhian's purposes admirably since she was there to observe rather than to be observed.

She spoke to several people as she descended from the upper terrace to the lower. There were two immense, green-striped tents. Under one was arranged a sumptuous buffet; the other covered a dance floor made of green and white marble tiles. Rhian smiled slightly at such an extravagance; it must have taken hours to level the ground with sand and lay the checkerboard tiles so they were flat and uniform. Around the gardens, servants were lighting flambeaux, creating pockets of bright light and intriguing shadows. She almost rubbed her hands with glee. The night should provide a wealth of material for her next Quidnunc column.

Rhian found a seat amongst the matrons and prepared for the show. She was glad she had brought a notebook and pencil in her reticule. She could slip away to the ladies' withdrawing room and jot down *bons mots* she overheard and record who danced with whom and how many times. And she was certain several strolls into the shadowy garden would garner innumerable delicious *on-dits* as well.

Rhian had discovered, since she had taken over the paper four years ago, that her best material came from masquerade balls and outdoor entertainments like this "breakfast" that would last till dawn. There were always trysts to uncover or imprudent young misses who went beyond the strict dictates of society. While Rhian didn't mention names, she would allude to certain events and that, she knew, created enough speculation to whet the appetites of the ton's busybodies and keep them all reading her paper. Some "facts" were common knowledge, and names were unnecessary, as in the case of the wager Lord Pembroke had made. But, as a rule, she tried to keep her stories accurate and anonymous, unless one already had access to the identities of the parties involved—which was usually the case where Society was concerned.

"My dear Lady Rhian, how good to see you. How is your dear father? Did he escort you this evening?"

Rhian pasted a polite smile on her face and responded, "No, Lady Holcomb. Father was otherwise engaged. He said he might drop in later this evening."

"Oh, I do hope so. He is such a dear man. And so handsome. Makes my heart flutter like a schoolgirl—I vow it does!"

"He is quite a charmer," said Rhian dryly. Her father was charming as long as he did not have to take responsibility for his actions. He liked nothing better than making a conquest, only to leave the lady dangling, wondering what she had done to spoil things. Still, judging by the number of covetous glances he earned, they continued to count the handsome lord with silver hair and bright blue eyes as eligible.

"Oh, my, there is Pembroke! I do hope he doesn't plan any outrageous behavior—for Lady Cowper's sake, to be sure," said Lady Holcomb, edging forward on her seat with a hopeful gleam in her eyes.

"Why Lady Cowper?" asked Rhian, pretending ignorance.

"Oh, hadn't you heard about his wager? The patronesses denied vouchers to Almack's to Mr. Sims's cousin. The news got about somehow and the poor thing has had to retire to the country. And all because she danced the waltz before receiving the permission of one of the patronesses. Pembroke vowed revenge on them all. He has managed to splash each one of them in the past two weeks, except Lady Cowper. It is rumored she defended the poor girl, so I daresay Pembroke will not wish to do anything rash."

"How do you mean—splash?"

Lady Holcomb looked around and leaned forward, allowing her fan to drop in front of her mouth. "I saw only one incident. It was in the park. Lady Jersey was promenading with Alvanley. Pembroke is such an excellent whip, he drove past, turning the horse in such a way that the wheel hit the puddle he was passing and gave her ladyship a thorough dousing. Didn't even touch Alvanley!"

Lady Holcomb sat back with a smug expression as though she were taking credit for the joke.

Rhian looked over at the viscount; she felt her face grow hot as he threw back his head and laughed at something his friends said. Mr. Sims, she knew, but the other gentleman was unfamiliar. She turned to her nosy neighbor and asked the short, round man's identity.

"Lord Chuffington. He is the one who took all wagers, betting that Pembroke would succeed. I daresay he is sorry now. Pembroke likes Lady Cowper too well to offer her insult. Oh, my, here she comes."

Rhian and Lady Holcomb—indeed, all eyes—turned to watch as Lady Cowper approached the trio of men. Mr. Sims and Lord Chuffington fell back, leaving the viscount to greet her ladyship alone.

"Good evening, my lady," he said, bowing over her proffered hand.

"My dear Pembroke. I understand you have been looking for me," said Lady Cowper graciously.

Jonathan's smile made Rhian clasp her hands in her lap nervously. He was such a handsome man, nothing like the effeminate dandies who dawdled their days away. He was dressed in black from head to toe, even his waistcoat. Only his cravat was white, and a black pearl winked from its folds.

The viscount bent his head to Lady Cowper and said something that made her smile and nod. Jonathan took two fingers and dipped them into his glass of champagne. Holding Lady Cowper's hand, he allowed a drop or two of the golden liquid to fall onto her glove.

Lord Chuffington let out a loud, "Huzzah!"

Jonathan bowed and escorted Lady Cowper to the dance floor where he led her out in the waltz just forming.

Rhian looked over at Lady Holcomb, amused by that lady's disappointment. Oh, this was too good! She was so glad she had come. The viscount was outrageous, but a gentleman, and very clever to have won his silly wager without disgracing the well-liked Lady Cowper.

It was just past midnight when Rhian slipped into the shadows and down a dimly lighted pathway. Her progress was soon arrested by a low voice on the other side of a tall hedge.

"Ah, my lovely!"

This pronouncement was rapidly followed by a shocked, "Lord Kent . . . please, take me back now! My mother . . ."

"But my dear girl . . ."

Rhian hurried down the path, looking for a spot to cross over. As she stepped into the next pathway, she saw not two silhouettes, but three.

The two men were of a size, but the one she knew to

be the lecherous Lord Kent was shrinking away, trying to fade into the darkness.

"Meant no harm, Miss North. Really, Pembroke, no need for melodrama. Your servant, Miss North," he mumbled before toddling away with an unsteady stride.

"Thank you, my lord," said the lovely, naive Miss North, batting her eyes for all they were worth.

Jonathan said, "My pleasure to be of service. Now, we must get you back to your mama." He guided the girl back to the light from the open lawn and released her arm.

Rhian watched as he propelled her toward the light, staying on guard until she had rejoined the other guests. Rhian slipped back into the darkened pathway as he turned. Passing within inches of her, she could smell his cologne.

The strains of a country reel floated toward her, and she turned back to the light. Pausing, she looked over her shoulder.

Shaking her head at her unaccustomed impetuosity, she pivoted and followed the handsome viscount. The cover of the shrubbery ended, and Rhian spied her quarry. He was facing the Thames, his hands clasped behind his back, his strong face and powerful figure in profile against the full moon. Rhian caught her breath as he turned back, his face etched in shadow. He seemed to be staring directly at her, and she froze.

Jonathan gazed at the house, lighted by flambeaux. Green Chinese lanterns winked at him from the garden. He smiled slightly as those green eyes invaded his thoughts for the hundredth time.

Who was she? he wondered again. He had to find her even if it meant attending every boring rout, literary salon, and ball during the Season. He would find her, and then, one way or the other, he would be able to settle his life into a comfortable routine once more.

He had tired of telling himself he would no longer be fascinated by her when he got to know her. He had told himself time and again that meeting her would put an end to his obsession. But deep inside, somehow he knew he would not only like her; she would complete him, and all the restlessness he had felt in the past four years since coming home from the war would be at an end.

Rhian remained motionless for several minutes after the viscount had returned to the breakfast. She was shaken by the roiling emotions in her breast, roused just from being close to a man—even such a man as Lord Pembroke. She took a deep breath; his cologne still lingered, and she suppressed a shudder.

This would not do, not at all, she told herself. She was content with her lot in life, not merely resigned. But this man had disturbed her equilibrium, knocking the wind out of her emotionally.

With a mental shake, she scolded herself for such foolishness. No man she had ever met was worth such upheaval. Undoubtedly, were she to become better acquainted with the viscount, she would be able to relegate him to the back of her mind, just like all the rest and get on with her life.

Having gone through two Seasons during her gangly teen years, she had seen the best the ton had to offer and had decided no one was worth giving up her independence for. Urged on by her late grandfather in this respect, she had retired from the glittering social whirl that was London and concentrated on the newspaper he had left to her. Since then, circulation had tripled, and she was kept very busy quietly gathering news and writing the social and literary columns. She had found happiness.

With another deep breath, Rhian took in the last wispy fragrance that the viscount had left behind. Closing her eyes and then grimacing, she fairly stalked back to the house. She bade her hostess farewell, her eyes straying to the handsome Lord Pembroke only once before making her escape.

A week passed and Jonathan grumbled as he stared at the jumble of crossed and re-crossed writing that had been his original outline. Pockets entered as was his custom around noon each day, and Jonathan glared at his friend.

"How's it coming?" said Pockets, cocking his fair head to one side with a mocking grin.

"Stubble it," growled the viscount.

"Not still having problems, are you? After all, it's just a silly novel—something any fool could write. I would have thought you'd have produced two or three by now."

Jonathan pushed back from the desk and stood up. "I've done enough for today. I'm going for a ride."

"Care for some company?" asked Pockets as his friend strode past.

"No, I don't."

Pockets's laughter followed Jonathan down the hall.

The scowl on Jonathan's face remained until he was out of London. He left behind the rumble of carriages and shouts of vendors and found his way to the quiet of a country lane.

Letting loose the reins, he allowed Neptune, his silver gelding, to canter down the side of the road.

He came to the tiny village of Westford and drew up in front of a small but respectable inn.

"Welcome back, my lord," said the landlord, a thin man with a drooping mustache.

"Thank you, Ivey. I hope you and your family are all well."

"Doing fine, m'lord. Just fine. My oldest made me a grandfather last week."

"Congratulations. Boy or girl?"

"Another girl, to be sure. That makes my eight plus the newest. I guess I'll only have sons-in-law, not sons. But I'm not complaining. My girls are jewels—real jewels."

"They are all very pretty and very sweet. Just like their mama," he added as the landlady came into the tap, wiping her hands on her apron.

"I thought it was you, my lord," she said, dropping a curtsey. "I've got a fine turkey roasting, if you're hungry."

"You know I am, Mrs. Ivey."

From behind her mother, a tow-headed little girl of five peeked at him.

"Make your curtsey to his lordship, Mimi," said her father.

She stepped out, smiled a toothless smile, and curtseyed quickly.

"Hello, Mimi. I've brought you and your sisters each a candy. Come here and hold out your hand."

The little girl did as she was bid, and Jonathan produced a handful of candy sticks from his pocket.

"Thank you, m'lord," she whispered before curtseying again and hurrying out the door.

"You're goin' to spoil them, m'lord," protested Ivey.

"I doubt it, Ivey. Besides, what else should a man do for his godchildren?"

"Now, you know we didn't ask you because we wanted you to be giving them handouts," said Ivey.

"Oh, Abe, don't go arguing with Lord Pembroke. After all, he's your old commander, and he's a good man. Now, I'll just run fix your luncheon, m'lord."

Jonathan accepted the tankard of ale offered and motioned to the chair opposite his. "Join me, Ivey."

The landlord sat down self-consciously, despite that Lord Pembroke and he had shared a great deal more than a tankard of ale when they were on the Peninsula together.

"I need your advice, Ivey," said Jonathan, his expression thoughtful.

"Mine, m' lord?"

Jonathan grinned. "Yes, pretend I am that green lieutenant who came to you on the Peninsula knowing absolutely nothing about commanding a troop of men, much less surviving without an army of servants."

"You mean the one with the high-strung stallion who didn't take to cannons?"

Jonathan chuckled at the remembrance. "I wonder whatever happened to him after he threw me and bolted."

"If he could 'ave run on water, I bet he's back in Ireland today."

They both laughed, and Ivey waited patiently for Jonathan to return to the original topic.

"I've made a wager . . ."

"Ah!"

Jonathan grinned. "Nothing so foolish as the ones I used to make. But this time, to win, I have to write a novel."

"That shouldn't pose any challenge for you, m' lord. You were always writing something."

"You'd think so, wouldn't you."

Jonathan stood up and paced the length of the room twice before stopping at the window and seeming to study the activity in the yard. Seven blond girls ranging from five to fifteen were laughing and playing.

"How did you feel when you met your wife?" he asked quietly.

"Feel? Ah, I see. Well, if I remember right, I was fairly bowled over. She was baking a pie in her mother's kitchen. Her mother was cook to Lord and Lady Pinkston. I was a new footman and came in to get the tea tray. She smiled at me. Ah, it was grand."

"Then you knew immediately?"

"I knew I wanted to get to know her."

"Yes, yes, that's it," said Jonathan. A thoughtful silence followed.

"You wanted to ask me something?" Ivey prompted finally.

"What would you have done if you'd been dismissed, unable to ever see her again. Would you have taken up with someone else?"

"Eventually, I suppose. But I would have moved heaven and earth to see her again first."

Jonathan returned to his chair. He leaned forward, his visage intense. "I've met someone."

"Congratulations, m' lord," said his old batman enthusiastically. He had worried his old master would never find happiness. But now . . .

"There is a problem. I don't know her name."

Ivey shot him an incredulous look. "But surely you can ask for an introduction, m' lord."

"Perhaps I should mention, I've only met her once, and no one remembers her." Jonathan proceeded to relate the strange events that led up to that carriage ride and magical smile. "Now I can't find her."

"Oh, that makes it difficult."

THE BLUESTOCKING'S BEAU

Both men fell silent until Ivey snapped his fingers. "You know, when I wanted to buy this inn, I placed an advertisement in the newspaper. That's how I came to find this place."

"A woman is very different from an inn," said Jonathan wryly.

"True, but you might be surprised. If the lady is of a literary bent, she might just spy the advertisement." When Jonathan said nothing else, Ivey added, "It may be a farfetched scheme, but I suppose it depends on just how desperate you are."

Jonathan grinned and said, "Pretty desperate."

Rhian spent the week after the breakfast avoiding the social whirl. Trying to regain an even keel, she threw herself into her work. But one morning her clerk Geoffrey brought her back to reality.

"My lady, have you written the Quidnunc column for tomorrow?" he asked confidently. Lady Rhian was always very conscientious about her work.

Rhian surprised him by flushing to the roots of her red hair. "Not yet," she said, shaking her head. It was the one thing she had not managed to produce.

The young man smiled and put a folded piece of paper on her desk. "You might want to include this little tidbit. It should cause quite a stir."

Rhian unfolded the paper, her color changing from red to white in seconds.

"My lady, are you all right?" asked Geoffrey anxiously. Incapable of speech, she merely nodded. "Let me get you some water." He stepped to a sideboard and poured her a glass of water.

Rhian sipped obediently. "Thank you, I'm fine now, just fine. I'll, uh, work on the column this evening. Tell Mr. Townsend to hold that space until last."

"Very well, my lady. Let me know if I can get you anything else."

The curious young man left the room, and Rhian opened the folded paper again. She tried to stem the rising excitement in her breast, but it was impossible.

He couldn't mean her! But he had to! She was the one who had "provided him transportation from the literary evening." And she had worn a turban that night.

Rhian willed herself to a sense of calm. Carefully, she read the advertisement one more time.

"Gentleman desires to locate turbaned individual who kindly provided transportation from Lady B's literary salon on the night of April 2. Please send response to:
Raymond and Ruggles, Solicitors
42 Lenox Road, London"

Rhian folded the note again and put it in her reticule. She wouldn't use it; it wouldn't do to turn her column into a matchmaking service.

She sucked in her breath in surprise. Matchmaking? Now she really was losing control. Why on earth should she assume the viscount's purpose was finding a. . . . Here, she paused in her thoughts. He wouldn't advertise for a wife. But what other conclusion was there? That the viscount would place such an advertisement showed how badly he wanted to find her.

But Rhian, as deeply as her attraction to the virile viscount might run, was not prone to romantic histrionics, and she forced herself to consider other possibilities. At first, none presented itself to her jumbled thoughts. Then, she snapped her fingers—a most unladylike gesture—and she stood up.

She replaced her dowdy hat and coat and left her office. "I'll be back tomorrow, Geoffrey, column in hand."

"Very good, my lady," he replied to the closing door.

Rhian made her way home quickly, hardly pausing at the back gate where the hackney driver let her down. She startled Angus by bursting into the mews and going straight to the old barouche.

"Maybe I kin help ye, m' lady. Wot is it yer looking for," said the gnarled old man, taking a step back as a carriage rug came flying at him.

"It's nothing, Angus. I have misplaced something," she lied.

"Perhaps I've seen it, m'lady."

She climbed down and said, "Perhaps you have."

"What is it, m' lady?"

Rhian flushed uncomfortably. "I'm not sure. It is actually a little trinket of a, uh, friend. I thought. . . . That is, she wondered if she had lost it in my carriage."

Though Rhian could tell from the groom's expression he couldn't recall any "friend" having been in the carriage, Angus had the grace to consider her explanation seriously.

"I didn't notice anything when I cleaned it. I think your friend must have lost it some place else, m' lady."

Rhian frowned. "You're sure no one else has been in it?"

"Not a soul," he said. "I allus look after this old beauty m'self, m' lady."

"Yes, I know. Well, I suppose I . . . that is, she was mistaken."

Having to content herself with this, Rhian sought the solitude of her room. Here her thoughts again ran rampant. If Lord Pembroke was not searching for her because he had lost something in her carriage, then why?

Rhian looked at her image in the glass. She pulled the pins from her long red hair and let it fall around her shoulders. She turned her head this way and that. Not bad, she concluded, not bad at all.

Except, she reminded herself, the viscount had seen the spinster Rhian with her hair hidden and her thick spectacles on—not to mention that atrocious gown. He couldn't possibly have formed an attachment to that Lady Rhian.

The only possible explanation for that advertisement was that he had lost something and wondered if it might be in her carriage. Setting aside her disappointment as being silly, Rhian sat herself down at her writing desk and began to compose the Quidnunc column. At the end, she included Lord Pembroke's advertisement. She would wait a few days before replying to the solicitors.

"What the devil is this?" asked Pockets, throwing a newspaper on top of Jonathan's desk.

Jonathan put down his pen and said dryly, "It appears to be a newspaper, old boy."

"Pray don't be obtuse. Read this," he said, stabbing at the Quidnunc column.

Smiling smugly, Jonathan read his advertisement. So, they had printed it despite the clerk's assurance that they did not do that sort of thing.

"Did you write that?" demanded Pockets more incredulous than ever as he watched his normally sensible friend continue to grin stupidly.

"Yes, I did."

"But Jonathan, only think! If the rest of the ton gets wind of this . . . or even if that girl sees it. . . . She might construe it as a . . . promise, of sorts. Surely you don't want to be forced into parson's mousetrap because of a silly infatuation! What if—"

"Don't worry. No one will know but you and I. And Green Eyes, of course, if she reads the column. And I hope she will."

"This is very unlike you, Jonathan," said Pockets.

"So is this," said Jonathan, frowning and picking up several sheafs of paper and handing them to Pockets. "And this, and this, and . . . this," he added, opening drawers that contained more used papers with line after line crossed out, rewritten, and crossed out again.

"I don't understand exactly what this has to do with that notice," said his friend.

"Don't you? Pockets, it is the most extraordinary, most damnable thing. I simply can't get past the opening in this silly novel. The hero and heroine have to meet, but nothing I turn out makes sense."

"But Jonathan, you're supposed to be writing a bad novel anyway."

"Perhaps, but I can't even manage that. I just can't get my characters together until . . ." Jonathan laughed bitterly at Pockets's incredulity. "Yes, you're probably right, maybe I've gone 'round the bend; no, undoubtedly I have. But I'm determined to meet Green Eyes. Absolutely determined."

* * *

Three days later, Jonathan found himself standing outside his solicitors, a piece of crumpled paper in his hands.

An anxious clerk, hovering behind him, said, "I'm sorry, m' lord. It was just a street urchin who delivered it. I wouldn't know him even if I saw him again."

"Nevermind."

Jonathan climbed back into his curricle and drove quickly through the busy streets. He pulled up outside the shabby building that housed the newspaper and threw the ribbons to his tiger. He glanced up and down the dirty street.

Handing over a small pistol, Jonathan said, "Use it if you have to."

"Yes, m' lord."

Entering the office, Jonathan barked, "Get me pen and paper, man."

Geoffrey bristled, but he produced these materials and stood back while Jonathan wrote and sealed his missive.

"See that your editor prints this in the next issue." Jonathan looked into the narrowed eyes of the clerk and added a grudging, "please," before stalking out the door.

Geoffrey tapped the paper against his palm thoughtfully. He shrugged and took the note into Rhian's office.

"That Lord Pembroke just left . . ."

"Pembroke?" squeaked Rhian, flying to the window in time to see his curricle disappear. Holding onto the windowsill, she sought a nonchalant tone as she inquired, "What on earth did he want?"

"He told me to give this to you."

She turned sharply. "To me?"

"To the editor," explained the clerk.

"Ah, very well." Rhian crossed the room and held out her hand. She was proud to note that her hand was steady.

Geoffrey placed it in her hand and waited for her to open it. "That will be all," she said. He nodded and left the room, his curiosity unsatisfied.

Rhian returned to her desk and sat down, her outward demeanor calm and collected. She laid the paper on the desk, staring at it as though it contained a spider.

She had never, not even as a silly young lady, felt such dread and anticipation. If the viscount had bothered to place another advertisement, then obviously he was not merely retracing his steps to find some lost trinket. And if this were so, if he were really searching for her . . .

Rhian stood up and began to pace the length of the room. Back and forth, back and forth, her disturbed gaze falling on the folded sheet of paper each time she passed the desk.

She was content. She didn't want her life compli- cated—especially by a man. Oh, but such a handsome, intelligent man, a treacherous inner voice pointed out. Yes, she responded, and also arrogant and domineering, like all men.

But even this thought could not stem the heat creeping into her limbs and traveling to the very epicenter of her traitorous body each time she glanced at that paper and recalled the handsome Lord Pembroke.

She stopped, picked up the missive, and unfolded it.

A flood of emotions washed over her, and she had to grasp the heavy desk for support. The warmth in her body turned to fire, and she sagged against the cool mahogany, her knees suddenly unable to support her.

"Rhian! you've done it again!"

"Mrs. Banyon, my lady," said an out of breath Geoffrey, following on the heels of Rhian's sister.

"Done what?" Rhian snapped, her flushed countenance frowning fiercely.

"Here!" she said, waving the latest edition under Rhian's nose. "You've given my greatest competitor a glowing review!"

"Your competitor? I didn't realize you were competing with Miss Austen," snapped Rhian who was in no mood for her sister's tantrum.

"You know what I mean! I won't stand for it any more! I've been patient, but this vindictive attack on every book that comes from my publishing house is intolerable. Even if you wish to hurt me, how can you disparage our grandfather's memory? He built that publishing house from nothing! And you're trying to tear down everything he ever accomplished!"

"I hardly think my reviews are the problem, Penelope."

"Oh! I know when I've been insulted! You mark my words, Rhian! I'll get even, one way or another." With this, Penelope sailed out the door.

"I'm sorry, my lady. I tried to stop her, but . . ."

Rhian wearily waved aside his apology. She handed him the paper and said, "See that this is added to tomorrow's edition."

Geoffrey read the paper and frowned. "Exactly as it is written?"

"Exactly."

"Very well, my lady." Shaking his head, he left the office.

He did not, however, take the phantoms with him, and they continued to haunt Rhian.

"Done what?" Rhian stopped, her dictatorial countenance
frowning fiercely.

Three

Events moved rapidly after Jonathan's second notice appeared in the newspaper. The ton had buzzed only mildly
over the first advertisement, but gossip over the latest was
now rife with hypotheses as to the author's identity.

At Almack's, that hallowed hall of matchmaking, hopeful mamas paraded their daughters and gossiped behind
their fans.

"I believe it was meant for my Margaret. We gave a
ride to a mysterious gentleman. It was after Lady Buff-
ington's rout," said one proud mama.

"Then it can't have been meant for her," replied another. "The first advertisement said April 2. You had not
even come to town by then. Now my dear Henrietta . . ."

And so the speculation progressed until, on the night
of Lord and Lady Newberry's ball, Rhian had to bite back
her amusement as she heard one guest after another quote
and misquote the two advertisements.

Though she, herself, had been forced to stay away from
her office because of curious spectators, Rhian had
memorized the second notice. Every word Jonathan had
penned was written on her mind.

"In reference to her letter of response, I am not
searching for an object, but for my turbaned rescuer
herself. Please respond to same address."

Rhian had at first told herself she should be insulted, that she should send a blistering message that she was not some lightskirt to be seduced by romance. But her honesty would not allow her to lie; she was flattered, and her interest was piqued. However, after long hours of deliberation, she had chosen not to respond, at least for the moment. She had decided to make the social rounds instead, observing Lord Pembroke objectively, and thus, hopefully recover from her nonsensical infatuation. So far, her strategy had not been effective.

"My dear Lady Rhian, there you are! Now where is your dear father? Do tell me he is here!"

"Yes, my lady. I believe he is in the card room."

"Oh, naughty man. He really shouldn't neglect us ladies so shamefully. I think I'll just go have a word with him."

Lady Holcomb sailed away, leaving Rhian with an amused expression on her face. This faded as she saw Jonathan enter the ballroom, lingering for a moment on the steps above before descending to the floor.

Rhian could not prevent the mercuric quickening of her heartbeat. She drank in every inch of his strong physique, from the broad shoulders to the muscular thighs and calves. His dress, as usual, was impeccable. Tonight he sported a coat of gray superfine that fitted like a glove. His waistcoat and pantaloons were black and his cravat was tied in the intricate mathematical. Those piercing, dark eyes swept the crowd. Rhian allowed herself a tiny sigh.

He would soon be dancing with one of the Season's reigning belles. Then he would spend a few minutes chatting and laughing with friends before dancing with one or two beautiful widows or matrons. Finally, he would either leave or retire to the card room.

Jonathan started her way, and Rhian slipped into a small alcove from which she could observe the dancers without drawing attention to herself.

Rhian looked down at her gown, a conservative cream with a navy overdress. Her one piece of jewelry was a short choker of pearls her mother had left to her; Penelope had received the rest. Her hair was pulled back in the usual severe chignon with a small lace cap settled on top; thick spectacles completed her image. She was very much the spinster, not at all the sort anyone would notice.

As she watched the dancers, Lord Pembroke in particular, Rhian found her feet moving to the music. Unaccountably, she wished she had an uncle or brother to lead her out for just one dance. She frowned fiercely at such a silly sentiment. Just then, Jonathan looked her way, his gaze flitting away immediately, his mind registering nothing at the sight of the plain spinster.

Rhian lowered her eyes, which had unexpectedly filled with tears. She took her handkerchief and surreptitiously wiped the corners of each eye. She thought she had been successful in suppressing false hopes, but she had obviously been deceiving herself if an unintentional cut could cause such pain. Rhian waited for the music to end. Then she rose and went to the ladies' withdrawing room to compose herself before telling her father she was ready to go home.

Jonathan bowed over the hand of the delectable Mrs. Underwood, a widow of indeterminable years whose dampened gown left little to the imagination. She was a witty, entertaining partner, and he usually enjoyed dancing with her, but his heart was not in it tonight. He wanted only to get away.

Of late, he had been wistfully thinking of his estate,

Silveroaks, wondering how the spring planting was going. He was losing all hope that he would ever find his Green Eyes, and without her, London had lost its luster.

Entering the card room, Jonathan caught sight of a familiar figure leaving the room by the far door. There was something about the way she held her head that reignited his hopes. The gown was fashioned in the old style with fitted waist and full skirt, revealing a tantalizingly curvaceous figure.

Jonathan stepped back into the ballroom only to see his quarry circling the far side of the dancers, heading toward the balcony. He followed as quickly as he could, weaving through the crush of elegant people.

When he reached the door to the balcony, he heard a blood-curdling scream. The music stopped; the dancers stopped. Jonathan bounded onto the terrace, his hand reaching automatically for his non-existent sword.

Others began to crowd outside also, and Jonathan found himself pushed forward until he was leaning precariously over the railing that overlooked a formal garden and a small ornamental pool.

In the pool, legs and petticoats waving and arms flailing, were a older man and a female he recognized as Lady Holcomb. The man managed to sit up, and he grasped the lady's hand and pulled her upright, also. He reached out a hand to straighten her bedraggled headdress before breaking into a drunken chorus of "We're A' Fu' ". The audience began to laugh and whisper. Servants came to the rescue of the mortified Lady Holcomb, who was crying by this time.

It was then that Jonathan saw his Green Eyes. She had lost her lace cap and her spectacles and presented a striking study of indignant fury and, to Jonathan, incredible beauty. Her anger made Rhian forget herself as she stooped to help her father to his feet.

"Father, do be quiet. You are making a spectacle of yourself! I have never been so ashamed!" she added more quietly now that she had his attention. She shrugged aside the servants and called for their carriage. With more dignity than Jonathan would have thought possible, she led her father through the ballroom, bade their host, (their hostess was prostrate on a settee), goodnight, and disappeared.

Jonathan took a step after her before common sense reasserted itself, and he thought better of it. He would have no difficulty discovering the identity of Green Eyes now. All he had to do was mention the gentleman who had gone for a swim in Lady Newberry's pond, and anyone would relate the name of the offender. And from there, he had only to ask about the daughter. Then . . .

A thought so horrendous occurred to Jonathan that he turned pale. What if his Green Eyes was married? What if she was not free? He was not the type to trifle with a married lady.

He turned to the person closest, a complete stranger, and asked anxiously, "Who was that gentleman?"

"That was Lord Ainsley, an aging roue with a penchant for strong drink, bad cards, and accommodating women," laughed his informant.

"And the girl?"

"Lady Holcomb?" asked the man doubtfully.

"No, the young one who read him a lecture."

"That? Oh, I think that must be his daughter, the one who is still unmarried," said his talkative neighbor while Jonathan heaved a sigh of relief. "Frightening sort of gel.

Much too independently minded for her own good, so I understand. Firmly on the shelf, of course."

Jonathan cut short more opinions and took himself off. He made his way to his club where he ascertained that Lord Ainsley was indeed a member, although he rarely could afford to gamble there anymore.

Jonathan whistled all the way home.

"I say, Jonathan, you haven't been up all night, have you?" asked Pockets when he joined Jonathan the next morning in the breakfast room.

Jonathan looked up, grinning. "I believe I have."

"Then what the deuce are you smiling about? I'm an absolute bear if I can't sleep at night."

"But you, Pockets have not just written the first third of your novel."

"First third?"

"Correct. Nor did you find out the identity of the lady you've been searching out for weeks," added Jonathan with a self-satisfied smirk.

"By Jove! So you finally ferreted her out. Who is she?"

"The daughter of Lord Ainsley. I didn't catch her name, but now that I know how to find her again, I'll make short work of that."

"Congratulations." Pockets helped himself to kidney pie and a steaming cup of coffee. Then he frowned and said, "But that still doesn't explain why you stayed up all night writing that novel. I mean, I know you had hardly even begun yesterday."

"I'd begun, time and time again. Unfortunately, nothing seemed to work. But now, the hero and heroine have met, and the rest is history, as they say. Or soon will be."

Pockets laughed at his friend, shaking his blond head. Then his fair brow wrinkled again, and he asked, "I say, Jonathan, you do remember that this is supposed to be a badly written novel, don't you?"

"Hm? Yes, yes, certainly. But it can at least have an element of truth and believability to it, can't it? Don't worry, I'm sure it will turn out every bit as bad as . . . That is, it's sure to be very dismal indeed. Now, I must get a little rest. I intend to track down Lord Ainsley, wherever he may be tonight, and wrangle an invitation to dine."

When Lord Ainsley appeared at breakfast the next morning, he wore an unexceptional dressing gown and a contrite expression. It was a familiar guise to Rhian and she accepted it without great enthusiasm.

"Good morning, my dear," he began cheerfully, though he blanched and quickly waved away the rasher of bacon and the eggs. "Fine morning. Do you fancy a drive through the park with me?"

"No, thank you, Papa. I'm afraid I have other plans today. But do go on without me. I would hate for you to be cooped up inside all day."

"Well, I suppose I could stop by the club . . ." He added quickly, "Just to meet with my friends and talk. Afterall, one can never be too well-informed about the events of the day. Yes, I think I'll just do that."

"Splendid, Papa. Enjoy your day."

Rhian went to the library and pulled back the curtains. The room overlooked the back gardens—if one could call the collection of overgrown flowers and shrubs a garden. But on this morning, with the sunlight streaming through the glass, it presented a cheerful picture.

The door opened, and her father cleared his throat.

"Yes, Papa?"

"I was wondering, my dear, I seem to have misplaced my purse . . ."

Rhian turned and went to her desk. She unlocked a drawer and produced a small roll of bills.

"Thank you, m' dear. Oh, by the way, I told Lady Holcomb and a few others that we were planning a small card party. Nothing extensive. Do you think you could speak to Tipton and Mrs. Gilbert?"

"When?"

"On Tuesday."

"I'll arrange it, Papa. Whom should I invite?"

"Just the usual, intimate little gathering. You're a splendid daughter, m' dear. I couldn't manage without you."

Her father left her alone again, and Rhian just shook her head. At least he was in a penitent state. She didn't have to worry about him losing what little he had left. She gave a silent thank you to her frugal grandfather once again for having given her the townhouse. At least her father couldn't lose it in a card game.

She sat down at her desk and began addressing the invitations.

Jonathan lost no time in securing an introduction to Lord Ainsley. He counted himself very lucky to have discovered him at their club. He was engaged in what should have been a desultory game of silver loo, but the intensity with which Ainsley played belied the small stakes and casual attitude. The man was as sober as a judge, too.

Jonathan sat down and proceeded to lose consistently. After several hours, Ainsley rose and challenged Jonathan to a game of piquet. Jonathan continued to oblige by losing very badly, much to the amazement of the rest of the company.

"My dear boy, I do hope you don't play for high stakes. You seem to have the most damnably bad luck."

"You should know, Ainsley," said one observer caustically.

"Indeed I should," said his lordship amiably, "but I would be remiss not to caution the boy."

Jonathan waved all this aside and reassured Lord Ainsley by saying, "I never lose more than I can afford."

"Then let's play on," said Ainsley, rubbing his hands together in anticipation. He was fairly beside himself. He had won enough to give Rhian back the money she had loaned him that morning—he always considered it a loan, although he had never repaid a penny. Of course, he amended, he would need a stake for the card game he was hosting on Tuesday, so he would just wait until Wednesday to repay Rhian. She wouldn't mind. She was such a good girl. And he was bound to win again then. He was on such a lucky streak!

Jonathan misplayed his card, and Ainsley shivered with anticipation. "I was wondering, my lord, if you'd care to come to my house for a little card party on Tuesday? I can promise you a congenial group."

Jonathan pretended to hesitate. "I'm not certain if I'm free. I'm staying with Mr. Sims, you know."

"Bring him along; the more the merrier," he said, laying down his hand. "That makes the rubber mine, I think." Lord Ainsley rose and said happily, "So we'll expect you and Mr. Sims on Tuesday, eight o'clock."

"I look forward to it," said Jonathan grinning at the enormity of his understatement.

* * *

Rhian had four days to prepare for the card party. This meant not only supervising the cleaning and polishing, but also participating in it actively. Supper would also be served, and this required hours of planning and preparation. Throughout it all, Lord Ainsley behaved admirably, never giving Rhian a moment's worry—a welcome turn of events Mrs. Gilbert and Tipton discussed daily.

Rhian still managed to write her column. She even read and reviewed one of the novels her sister had published. The review was not glowing, but it was warm enough that Penelope sent Rhian a note congratulating her on her caution. Since Rhian had never had the slightest inclination to succumb to her sister's threats of exposure, she read the note angrily. Tearing it up made her feel better, but she wished she had more time. She would have written Penelope a very telling rebuttal. As it was, Tuesday was flying toward her, and she had much too much to accomplish.

"Shut up, Pockets," growled Jonathan, running his finger around his collar which seemed much more constrictive than usual.

"I can't help it, old boy. I've never seen you nervous before. Why, even facing the fiercest of Napoleon's guard, you never let slip your fortitude. But tonight, just the thought of encountering that slip of a girl has you all aquake," said Pockets, reaching out to make a minute adjustment to Jonathan's tie. "There we are. Now you're all presentable."

"Shut up," said Jonathan again.

"And so eloquent, too," said Pockets, holding up both hands as if to ward off a blow. They rapped on the door sharply and waited what seemed an age before Howard opened it and let them inside.

"Come in, gentlemen. Let me show you to the salon," he said formally after reading their cards.

Jonathan let Pockets go first. As eagerly as he had anticipated this moment, he felt every bit the foolish schoolboy. His palms were moist, and his brow damp.

Howard announced them and backed away. Jonathan's gaze swept the room; he wanted to groan, but he didn't. Rhian was nowhere to be seen. Instead, it appeared to be a room of older people. He and Pockets were the youngest guests present.

Lady Rhian Ainsley wasn't even there!

Turning to greet their host, Jonathan refrained from demanding that he produce his daughter. Pockets, on the other hand, couldn't contain himself.

"Where's your daughter, my lord? I would like to pay my respects to her; we frequent the same literary salons."

"Don't doubt that for a minute," he said jovially. He lowered his voice and added, "Always has her nose in a book! Bit of a bluestocking, though I am loath to admit it about my own daughter."

"Is she here tonight?" asked Jonathan, unable to stop himself.

"Yes, she's around the house someplace. No doubt she'll put in an appearance later, just to make sure everyone is being entertained."

Jonathan and Pockets exchanged frustrated looks before joining the other guests.

Before long they had been paired with partners and found chairs at the various tables set up around the room.

Glasses were filled, cards shuffled and dealt, and the play
began. Jonathan found himself facing the far wall, a matron of undeterminable years his partner. Opposing them
were Lady Holcomb and Lord Ainsley, who had every
intention of continuing his rout of the unlucky Lord Pembroke.

An ancient butler toddled around from time to time
replenishing glasses, but there was no sign of Rhian.
Jonathan, in a temper, began to play his usual game.
Soon, Lord Ainsley was frowning and drinking much
more than he should have. His voice grew in volume,
as did his wagers.

Rhian looked up from the book she was reading. "What
is it, Tippy? Everything going all right?"

The butler shook his head worriedly. "Your father has
asked me to go back down to the cellar for more brandy."

Rhian frowned. "Is he disguised?"

"I'm afraid so, my lady."

She stood up and patted his frail shoulder. "Don't
worry. I'll take care of it."

Rhian smoothed her green gown of watered silk and
walked calmly to the salon. She spoke to several guests
as she made her way across the floor.

Pockets, facing the door, spied her first. He coughed
loudly. Jonathan glanced up sharply as Pockets urgently
inclined his head toward Rhian.

Jonathan watched, enchanted, as she leaned down to
whisper into her father's ear. She was smiling graciously,
very conscious of her audience. Then she looked into
Jonathan's eyes and fell silent.

"You're right, of course, my dear. We should go in to
supper. It's almost midnight." He stood up and held out
his arm to Lady Holcomb who simpered and sidled up

beside him. Jonathan's partner waited in vain for him to extend his arm and finally went off in a huff.

Rhian and Jonathan stood mesmerized as the rest of the guests cleared the salon. Smiling, Pockets closed the doors.

Jonathan circled the table slowly, his tread measured as he stepped closer and closer. Rhian's eyes widened as he took her arm and started to lead her to the garden doors. Rhian hesitated on the doorsill. With a slight smile, Jonathan took both her hands in his and calmed her uncertainty.

Rhian followed.

Part Two
The Waltz

Four

Under the full moon, in the midst of the overgrown garden, Jonathan gazed at her, his heart in his eyes. Rhian's breath was shallow and rapid. She watch him carry her hand to his lips and kiss her fingertips. She closed her eyes, shuddering. Jonathan stepped closer and lifted her chin, willing her to open those glorious green eyes again. His mouth came down on hers, touching her lips tenderly. When she swayed toward him, he caught her in his arms, his touch like fire on her skin. Rhian tilted her head back, her gaze of amazement causing Jonathan to smile. He kissed her again, this time more urgently, and Rhian met his demand, her passion stirred in a manner so new, so wondrous, all indecision was swept away with each new kiss, each tantalizing caress. His tongue teased her lips and, her eyes opening wide, penetrated her mouth. Exhilaration chased away surprise, and Rhian moaned, molding her body against his.

Jonathan knew his control was slipping; with an effort born of love, he raised his mouth and relaxed his embrace—not too much, or Rhian would have crumpled to the ground. He looked around, spied a bench in the jungle of a garden, and led her to it.

When they were seated, he covered her hands with his

and said, "You didn't answer my second advertisement. Didn't you see it?"

"I saw it."

"But you didn't want to meet me?" he asked, holding his breath lest her answer destroy him.

Rhian's lips curved dreamily. "I couldn't allow myself to believe it."

"Do you believe it now?"

She nodded, and he smiled, raising her hand and kissing her palm.

They sat in silence for several moments, a comfortable quiet which both were loath to break. Finally, Jonathan rose and helped her to her feet.

"Do you feel equal to returning to the company?" he asked.

"Yes, we should go inside."

"We must get to know each other. You'll go for a drive with me tomorrow?"

Rhian nodded and, astonished at her own boldness, raised her lips for another kiss. Jonathan grinned and obliged with a quick buss before taking her hand and returning to the house.

Rhian waited impatiently for Fanny to finish brushing her hair. Her body quivered with excitement, and she wanted to avoid questions. For this night, she wanted to hug her delicious secret to herself.

"That will be all," she said rather sharply, earning a flash of curiosity. She knew Fanny would be delighted at her good fortune, but she didn't want to share it yet.

"Very good, my lady," said the servant when no excuse was forthcoming.

Rhian stood up and floated across the room; she paused at the window, looking out at the gaslights around the square. A lone figure stood beneath one, and her heart leapt. Then the figure walked away; it was not her . . .

Her what? she asked herself.

But Rhian was much too happy to bother with doubts and questions. Love and lust raced through her and for that night, for the first time in her twenty-four years, she allowed it free reign.

Where would this lead? asked a cautious voice.

Rhian fell into bed and snuggled beneath the counterpane.

Out loud, defiantly, she said, "I don't care!"

Jonathan made his way home with Pockets, his heart light, a fatuous smile residing firmly on his face.

"What now?" asked Pockets, attempting to inject a voice of reason into Jonathan's happiness.

"Now? Now we see what may come. In the meantime, run on to bed, or to the club, or wherever. I've got writing to do."

Jonathan made his way upstairs to his room and writing desk. He repaired the point of his pen and dipped it in the inkwell. "Chapter Two," he wrote.

The sun was turning the sky a rosy pink before Jonathan stood up and stretched his stiff muscles. He glanced at his watch and shook his head. The thirty pages he had produced had flowed like water, his pen moving rapidly to keep pace with his imagination.

Jonathan smiled. He had never considered himself a man of great imagination, but Green Eyes—Rhian—had awakened a creature in his breast he rarely encouraged.

He had spent his life doing what was expected and required of him. He had pleased his tutors, excelled at school, and followed this with a distinguished career at Oxford. Finally, restless and reckless, he had bought a commission in the army to fight the French where he had often earned mention in dispatches. One of the fortunate ones, he returned unscathed. His father gone, he had taken over the running of his estate, turning it into one of the most progressive and prosperous in all of England.

But that winter, at the ripe old age of thirty-two, an unfamiliar boredom had gripped him, and he had seized the opportunity to spend the Season in London. Jonathan had been perfectly content with the occasional social function, punctuated by boxing at Jackson's, shooting at Manton's, and gambling at White's or Watier's.

Then Green Eyes had entered his life, his very soul, and Jonathan knew things would never be the same.

He threw himself down on the bed and willed himself to sleep. He had only a few hours to wait before he would be with her again. On this thought, he fell asleep, the perpetual half-smile curving sensually.

"Lord Pembroke, my lady," announced Tipton formally as he showed Jonathan into the salon. In the morning light, a quick glance showed the timeworn furnishings, but then his black eyes found Rhian and all else was forgotten.

She was seated on a sofa, her dark green gown setting off the fiery red hair and bright emerald eyes to perfection. Jonathan joined her, lifting her hand to his lips for a gallant kiss.

"Good morning, my lord," said Rhian shyly, willing her racing pulse to stabilize. This didn't seem likely since he retained her hand in his, sending a delicious warmth tripping through her body.

"I'm Jonathan. I know it is forward of me, but I feel I've known you for a long time. You've hardly left my thoughts since that first night."

Rhian smiled, but she couldn't let such an absurdity pass. "Come now, my . . . Jonathan, you didn't even know my name."

He chuckled and sat back on the sofa, totally at ease. "Perhaps, but believe me, once I decide to accomplish something, like discovering your identity I never rest until I've managed it. My nurse used to tell me I was born obstinate."

"My father has said much the same thing. He says my head is as hard as a diamond." She looked into his eyes and smiled, saying, "But as my sister would lecture, I shouldn't be revealing such unbecoming traits to a suitor." She blushed a deep rose and stammered, "That is a, uh, visitor."

Jonathan retrieved the hand she had just put to her mouth and kissed it again. "Suitor is a perfectly acceptable word in this case." Rhian thought her heart would burst with joy. Then Jonathan stood up and said, "Let's go for that drive. We've been given the blessing of a beautiful day, although it is a little chilly. You'll probably need a cloak."

Rhian put on a lightweight green wool cape and set her bonnet on her head, tying the ribbons at a jaunty angle. She knew very well no fashionable lady would be caught dead covering her gown with such a sensible garment when driving with a gentleman, but she didn't care if Jonathan didn't.

Rhian held onto the seat as they drove rapidly through

the busy streets. When they reached the park, she held on tighter still as he sprang the horses. It only lasted a minute or two before he pulled them to a reasonable trot, but Rhian's face was flushed with exhilaration.

"You are an excelled whip, Jonathan," she said admiringly. "I have read about your prowess with the ribbons, but I have never seen you drive before."

"And you approve?"

"If I didn't, I would have asked to be set down. But it was obvious, even to a ham-handed driver like I am, that you would not overset us. I felt quite safe."

"Good, I wouldn't want you to try and escape," he said, giving an evil laugh.

Rhian giggled like a schoolgirl, surprising herself by the uncharacteristic outburst. She sounded like a silly debutante. But Jonathan hadn't noticed.

"So you drive, too?" he asked, flicking his whip delicately over the leader's ear.

"Yes, I have a gig, though it's nothing compared to yours. And my horse Rabelais is getting on in years. But he understands me and doesn't complain when I'm a little heavy-handed."

"Do you ride as well?"

"No, I don't have a riding hack," she said, knowing full well it wouldn't have mattered if she had. She had been afraid to ride since she was a little girl. But she didn't want Jonathan to think her craven.

"If you'd rather ride one day, I just bought a lady's mount for my niece, but I haven't sent the mare down to her yet. The exercise would do her good."

"Perhaps we can," she said noncommittally. Rhian didn't wish to pursue this line of conversation any further and decided to switch to a safer social topic.

"Have you been to Drury Lane to see Edmund Kean play Shylock, the role that made him famous?"

"Not yet, but I do like Shakespeare. I was hoping you might accompany me this week."

"Oh, I didn't mean to be hinting," said Rhian, horrified that she had forced him into an awkward position.

Jonathan hastened to reassure her. "I know that. But I would love it if you would go with me. We'll ask your father as well, if you wish."

"That's not necessary," said Rhian, unwittingly endearing herself to him by her innocence.

She seemed to have no idea that she shouldn't be alone with him in his box. When he mentioned this to her, she looked puzzled.

"I don't see why not, Jonathan. I go wherever I please without incurring anyone's censure."

"Perhaps before, when you were wearing that silly cap and those dreadful spectacles, but not now. That reminds me, where are they?"

"What?" she asked.

"Those horrible spectacles."

"Oh, I only wore them so I would be left alone. They are just clear glass."

He laughed and teased, "They worked admirably, to be sure. But now, you'll be causing heads to turn if you are seen in my company, and while I don't care for myself, I do care for your reputation."

Rhian smiled and said, "I'm afraid I have grown used to thinking myself past the need for chaperons and such. But I thank you for thinking of it."

"My pleasure. Now, who can we . . ." He snapped his fingers, causing his horses to crabstep daintily. He pulled them back into line easily. "Pockets has the most fierce-looking aunt, and she is in London for the Season."

"Fierce?" said Rhian, frowning.

"Don't worry. Aunt Rosie is really as friendly as a little hedgehog, but she looks more like a bull dog. You'll like her, and since I intend to take you everywhere, we may have use of her on more than this occasion. As a matter of fact, are you going to Almack's tomorrow night?"

"Almack's?" she squeaked, knowing full well how he had angered the patronesses since she had recounted the details in her Quidnunc column. If they were still angry, she was liable to lose her vouchers if found in his company. And she needed the entree into Almack's to gather the best social news. But the expectation of a waltz with Jonathan chased away her doubts, and she nodded eagerly.

"Good! We'll go to Grillon's for supper afterwards. The refreshments at Almack's are too paltry to consider. And I'll bring Aunt Rosie to meet you this evening if you're going to be home."

"Yes, I planned to spend a quiet evening," she said, thinking of the work she needed to do.

Jonathan drew rein and leapt to the ground, throwing the ribbons to his tiger. He reached up for her, circling her waist with strong hands and swinging her down. Hand in hand, they strolled along a narrow path in silence.

Pausing beside a small pool covered in waterlilies, Jonathan asked, "Do you like living in London?"

"Yes, it has been several years since we lived in the country. There is an estate, but it is neglected. When I was a child we lived there, but my mother was alive then, and things were very different. Wherever she was, everyone was happy. Even my father. When she grew ill, it was much more difficult and lonely." Rhian shook off her gloom and turned to face him, asking, "Do you like London?"

"London is very entertaining, but when one is accustomed to the quiet of the country, it is also unsettling. So I shall definitely be glad when it is time to go home. I miss Silveroaks."

"Oh," was all Rhian could think to say.

He smiled down on her, his hand reaching up to stroke her cheek. He bent his head and kissed her lightly.

"You'll like Silveroaks," he said warmly. "In the summer, when London is sweltering, there is always a cool breeze. And if it does get hot, there will be an afternoon shower to cool things off. On the east side of the house, there is a terrace where I always have breakfast; the rising sun shines through the trees, gently warming the stone floor. It is simply splendid. For tea, you can't find a better spot than the gazebo by the lake. When London gets thin of company, we'll move to Silveroaks. I'll ask my mother to come over from Bath. She'll want to meet you."

Rhian knew she should protest, she should at the very least advise caution. But the picture he painted was too delightful to destroy with calm reason. So she smiled and allowed him to kiss her again, this time lacing her fingers around his neck and pressing against him in an indecently luscious embrace.

Rhian slipped out the back gate and into the waiting hackney. Rather than risk being spotted in her own gig, she now engaged the hackney to take her to the office every morning and pick her up in the afternoon.

Today, the driver set off at a smart pace, having been informed that his passenger would need to be home early to go out for the evening. It seemed there was suddenly a man involved in her ladyship's life. He prided himself on knowing all about the gentry's movements before they did. He was a very downy cove.

When Rhian climbed down, he tipped his hat and said, "I'll be back at four o'clock, my lady."

"Thank you," she said, wondering how he had read her mind.

Rhian ran up the steps and inside the neat building. She greeted Geoffrey before hurrying into her office. When he entered a few minutes later, she was sorting through the mail. Geoffrey cleared his throat noisily.

"Yes, Geoffrey. What is it?"

"It appears we have started a trend, my lady." He added a stack of envelopes to the pile on her desk.

Rhian frowned and opened the one on top.

"Dear Sir, please accept this plea for publication in your newspaper. Wanted: one hard-working female to mother my children. Willing to pay settlements for the right candidate. Leave message at The White Horse on Minden Lane, London."

"Geoffrey, this is outrageous!" said Rhian.

"That's just the first one," said the clerk, grinning.

"What, are they all like this?"

"All of them, though some are less straightforward. I was that surprised."

"So am I. I never dreamed . . ."

"But whatever shall we do about them? You can't mean to publish them."

"No, I don't want to turn our little paper into a lost lovers column. But I hate to simply ignore all these. We could lose subscribers over something like that," said Rhian. Geoffrey shuffled his feet uncomfortably. "What is it?" she asked.

"I talked to Mr. Townsend about it."

"And?"

"He thinks you might do a special edition that is just a broadsheet, really, of advertisements like this."

"Do you think we should?"

"I think it might be done tastefully; we could present it as a service, you know, to our loyal readers."

"You may be right. But do we have enough material?"

"Why don't you mention it in the Quidnunc column for tomorrow? That would bring in enough to fill two broadsheets!"

Rhian grinned. She liked the idea of helping others to find the happiness she was experiencing. She was not naive enough to believe all the people writing to the newspaper would be so lucky, but she wanted to give them a chance, at the very least.

"We'll do it. Let me just finish up the column, and Mr. Townsend can have it. Oh, and Geoffrey, I won't be in tomorrow at all. I've simply got to go shopping."

Geoffrey raised his eyebrows; never in three years had he heard his employer talk about shopping, except perhaps to ridicule some spendthrift in the Quidnunc. He bowed slightly and backed out of the room. Something, he thought, was definitely afoot.

That evening, Rhian dressed with extra care, knowing Jonathan was bringing by Mr. Sims's aunt to meet her. She wanted to look her best for Jonathan, and she was very mindful that her gown was several seasons old and

a trifle short, as well. The color, a dull burgundy, was very
elegant, but she suddenly wished she hadn't taken the time
to go to the newspaper that afternoon. She wished she
had visited the modiste instead. Rhian chuckled to herself;
she wondered what had happened to eradicate the old
Rhian so quickly and so thoroughly.

Her hair was piled on top of her head, much to the
delight of Fanny, who had been given free rein to create
a fashionable style for once. Little tendrils escaped around
the neck and in front, softening the stubborn jawline. The
effect was startling. Rhian looked at her image again.

The last time she had really noticed her appearance had
been four years ago when she had decided she would
never marry. Having read the works of Mary Wollstone-
craft, she firmly believed in feminine independence, so
the decision had not been difficult at the time. She had
scoffed at the other young ladies so wrapped up in their
appearances and social contacts. They dreamed of
fairytales, but most ended up subjugated and learned to
get their own way through deceit and manipulation.

Now, the young woman who stared back at her was not
the thin, gauche girl whom she had turned her back on.
In her place was a self-confident, mature lady. Then,
forced to wear gowns of white or pale pastels, her skin
had appeared sickly; now, in the jewel tones she preferred,
it was translucent. Though she felt certain one wouldn't
label her a beauty, she was definitely more appealing than
before.

Before you met Jonathan Stirling, teased an inner voice.
Rhian smiled, her green eyes lighting in amusement. She
tilted her head to one side, staring intently at the smiling
reflection; now that, she thought, was even better.

"My lady, Lord Pembroke is here with another gentleman and a lady."

"Thank you, Fanny, I'm coming."

Rhian had to force herself to walk down the stairs calmly, denying her instincts to run. She entered the salon, her eyes searching him out quickly and a smile forming immediately.

How handsome he was! she thought for the hundredth time. His black coat fitted like a glove, and his muscular thighs filled the knitted breeches most sensuously. His black hair, cropped short and combed into an endearing disarray, made her want to pull his head down to hers. She blushed at the thought, and Jonathan had the audacity to leer at her as though reading her mind.

He came forward and took her hand, placing it on his arm possessively. There was a time when this would have angered her, but again, with Jonathan, nothing was as it had been before.

"Allow me to introduce you to Miss Primrose Fairchild. Miss Fairchild, Lady Rhian Ainsley."

Rhian dropped a quick curtsey to the older lady and sat down by her side on the sofa.

"So good to meet you, Lady Rhian. Jonathan has told me all about you. He is such an impetuous boy," said the white-haired septuagenarian. She shook her finger at Jonathan. "I told him he couldn't rush young ladies, but now that I see you, my lady, I can understand his impatience." She leaned closer to Rhian as if to confide, "I daresay you'll do him a world of good."

"Thank you, Miss Fairchild."

"Please, if I'm to be your chaperon, you must call me Aunt Rosie. All the children do."

Rhian tossed a quizzical glance at Jonathan and Pockets.

Pockets laughed and explained, "My Aunt Rosie had a hand in raising all the children in the neighborhood, Jonathan included. We loved visiting her cottage. Most summers were spent there."

"Oh, it's a lovely spot, right in the middle of a forest. I have ducks, sheep, cows, ponies, and pigs."

"I hope I'm not keeping you from home," said Rhian hastily.

"Goodness, no. I also have a house here, and I come up for a month or two each spring. I was delighted when Jonathan and Clive asked me to help out. There's nothing I like better than being among a group of youngsters!" she declared stoutly with a fond look for all three of them. "Ah, I see your very efficient Tipton has brought the tea tray. Shall I pour out?" she asked before setting about performing this task. "You see, I love to be the one who pours. That way, I can slip all the sugar I want into my own cup without anyone else noticing." So saying, she put six lumps of sugar into her cup and stirred it gently.

"Aunt Rosie has a bit of a sweet tooth," said Pockets.

"There's nothing wrong with that," replied Rhian politely, smiling at the older woman.

"Good girl!" said the old woman, her blue eyes twinkling with approval.

They stayed over an hour, not at all an acceptable first visit socially, but everyone was having such fun, no one noticed the time.

Lord Ainsley looked in around nine o'clock, just as he was going out. Seeing Miss Fairchild, he entered and proceeded to charm her as he did all the older women. Rhian's expression became reserved. When her father finally excused himself, she breathed a sigh of relief.

Aunt Rosie patted her hand and said consolingly, "Take

heart, my child. At least he doesn't wish to always be in your pocket as my father did. I swear, that's why I didn't marry. The gentlemen never could get past my doting father. Now, we really must be going, boys. We've stayed longer than is proper as it is. Jonathan tells me he wishes to take you to Almack's. Eat well before you go; the refreshments are unbearable and scant."

"I shall," said Rhian, sharing her amusement with Jonathan who wagged his finger at her as if giving a scold. The gesture disappeared rapidly when Aunt Rosie turned to take his arm.

"Good-bye, my dear," she said, presenting her cheek for a kiss.

Rhian hid her surprise and obliged. Then she asked hesitantly, "I was wondering, Miss . . . Aunt Rosie, if you would care to go shopping with me in the morning? I know it's rather short notice . . ."

"I'd love to! Oh, what fun we'll have. Why, I haven't had the dressing of a young lady since Clive's older sister was presented ten years ago. I can hardly wait! Shall we say ten? I can't abide slugabeds when there is shopping to do!"

"Ten will be fine. I'll call . . ."

"No need, I'll pick you up. My servants don't have enough to do anyway with only me to look after. See you at ten!"

Jonathan lingered by the door until Pockets and his aunt had left. Then he swooped down to kiss her mouth, a lightning touch that left them both craving more. But there was no time.

"I'll see if I can come, too, shall I?"

"That would be lovely," said Rhian, surprising herself again.

"Good night, my love."

Rhian's mouth dropped open, but he was gone, and she had no one to ask if she had heard aright. Hugging herself, she performed a pirouette around the room, coming to rest at the pianoforte. Sitting down, Rhian played a lively piece by Haydn, her efforts enthusiastic, if not precise.

Jonathan put down his pen as the clock chimed four. He stretched wearily. Another productive night, he thought, sighing with satisfaction. Another few weeks and he would be finished with this blasted novel.

But it is not a "blasted" novel, he admitted. Instead, it had taken on a life of its own. He had no illusions that it was any good; after all, what did he know about writing a novel? He had always been too busy sorting through the lives of Plutarch and such to analyze what made a good story. But if his heart could make the novel come to life, then it would breathe passion and excitement, for these were the emotions which now filled him—now that he had found his Green Eyes.

He chuckled when he thought about what he would be doing in a few short hours, playing footman to two ladies bent on shopping all day. His friends at White's and Manton's would have a heyday with that one. It would probably be mentioned in that gossip column:

"Lord P was seen trailing after two ladies, in Bond Street. One supposes he hopes to be thrown a bone."

Still wearing his dressing gown, Jonathan fell into bed and sleep. His dreams were wild and strange with Rhian playing the heroine to his hero.

* * *

At ten o'clock precisely, Aunt Rosie's luxurious carriage pulled up in front of Rhian's town house. Jonathan jumped down and sprinted up the steps. Rhian, unlike any other female of his acquaintance, was waiting in the hall, bonnet in place and gloves in hand.

"Good morning, my lord," she said a little breathlessly.

"My lady," he replied with a bow, conscious of the footman and butler looking on. He held out his arm and she took it. "You look very beautiful this morning. I could wish the weather were better, but you make the day shiny despite the rain."

Rhian blushed at his fulsome compliments, but she was pleased, and she couldn't doubt his sincerity. His dark eyes gave away everything.

Their first stop was a modiste of considerable fame and outrageous prices. Rhian allowed herself to be draped and pinned until she was ready to drop. In the end, however, she ordered only one gown, the cost so dear she blanched at the thought. From there, they went to a more humble shop which she frequented. The owner, a soft-spoken French emigré, was eager to please a regular customer, especially one accompanied by such influential friends. She produced several models and lengths of cloth which Aunt Rosie and Rhian agreed were positively essential.

They took a break from their rigorous shopping at Gunter's and had ices. Jonathan ordered champagne as well, much to Aunt Rosie's delight.

"So gallant, so romantic," she whispered loudly to Rhian who looked into Jonathan's compelling eyes and smiled.

Aunt Rosie pronounced the expedition a prodigious

success, and proceeded to entertain both Rhian and Jonathan with tales of her own debut fifty years earlier when lace and powdered wigs were in fashion.

"There was one young man, (he later became Lord Hampton), who was quite taken with me. He was too fond of the bottle for my taste. One evening we had been dancing, and when it ended, he tried to kiss me in the middle of the ballroom. I was shocked, needless to say, and pushed him back. His hand caught my wig and sent powder all over his blue coat. Another inebriated young man demanded satisfaction, and they drew swords right there in the ballroom."

"What did you do?" asked Rhian, thoroughly intrigued.

"Oh, my, I was such a silly gudgeon back then," she replied, her gentle laughter causing others nearby to turn and smile. "Instead of leaving them alone—for truth be told, they would probably have passed out before either one could land a blow—I threw myself between them, lost my balance, and clutching wildly, threw all of us to the floor."

"Then what happened?" laughed Jonathan, his eyes never leaving Rhian's face.

Aunt Rosie lowered her voice, and said, "I was sent home in disgrace, but I'll never forget that night. Oh, what a memory we made!"

By five o'clock, they were finished, Rhian the proud owner of one gown suitable for Almack's and several more that were to be sent home by the end of the week.

As they pulled up outside her house, Rhian said, "Won't you come in for tea?"

Jonathan brightened, but Aunt Rosie dashed his hopes, saying, "No, my child we must be going if I am to be ready in time for tonight's festivities. I must have a little lie down," she confided. With a cheery wave, she said, "We'll call for you at nine."

Jonathan helped Rhian down, lingering by the door until called back by Aunt Rosie. She rapped his arm with her fan and laughed.

"You, my boy, are most well and properly caught by cupid's arrow, that is plain to see. She is a very intelligent young lady; she suits you perfectly. How long before you and she set the date?"

"We've only just found each other, Aunt Rosie. Give me time; I don't want to frighten her away."

The older lady stuck her nose up in the air and said haughtily, "And I thought you were a man of action, Jonathan Stirling. Take my advice and see that you don't waste too much time. You have awakened a beautiful butterfly from her cocoon. In no time at all, you'll find yourself standing in line to beg a dance. Mark my words."

Five

In the past four years, Rhian only attended Almack's for one purpose, to gather information for her Quidnunc column. It was there, in those modest rooms, where marriages and reputations were made and lost, all within the movements of a few dances.

But tonight, dressed in her new emerald silk with the high waist and the flowing skirt, her hair arranged *a la grecque,* and her shining eyes without thick spectacles, she seemed to be seeing it anew. And the other guests, judging from the number of fans going up to hide chattering mouths as they passed by, were seeing Lady Rhian Ainsley in a new light.

"Radiant," said Jonathan, speaking softly in her ear. "That's the only word that applies to you, my dear."

Rhian felt warmth spreading rapidly to every nerve in her body as she returned his look of admiration. "And you, Jonathan, are the most handsome man here tonight," she whispered, wondering at her own temerity.

But he was pleased by her remark, just as she had been by his. He presented her to Lady Cowper and her escort, Aunt Rosie's old beau, Lord Hampton. Rhian managed to keep her wicked thoughts to herself. Then Jonathan begged permission for Rhian to waltz.

The patroness looked puzzled. "I'm sorry, my lord, but

I'm sure Lady Rhian has received our permission in the past."

Though Lady Cowper was much too well-mannered to say it, her implication that Lady Rhian was well past the age to ask anyone's permission to do anything, struck Lord Hampton as funny. Laughing, he hastily excused himself and proceeded to spread the joke throughout the company.

Jonathan's blazing anger caused Lady Cowper to apologize, but Rhian said sensibly, "There is no need, my lady. You are not to know I haven't danced in several seasons, so I have yet to have the opportunity to waltz."

Lady Cowper smiled at her graciously, and said, "Then I will certainly give you permission, my lady. And may I add, Lord Pembroke is lucky to have found such a delightful partner."

"Thank you, my lady."

"Thank you," echoed Jonathan.

The music began, and Jonathan swept Rhian onto the dance floor with a graceful turn. He held her more closely than decency allowed, but Rhian didn't care. As a matter of fact, she wished he would hold her tighter. She wished they were alone, out in the garden again, away from prying eyes . . .

"A penny for your thoughts, my dear," said Jonathan, his deep voice sending shivers down her spine. At her blush, he gave a low laugh. "Too lascivious to vocalize, I'll be bound."

Rhian opened those green eyes wide, pretending indignation. Then she smiled, her expression decidedly provocative. "You, my dear Jonathan, are a great deal too perceptive."

This caused him to shout with laughter, and all eyes turned in their direction. Rhian expected him to relax his hold around her waist, but he merely held her closer, their bodies almost touching as he twirled her round the floor.

Giddy from the exercise and from her emotions, Rhian wished she could lay her head on his broad shoulder, but she managed to tame this desire.

When the music ended and they had finished their promenade, Jonathan returned her to Aunt Rosie and went in search of refreshments for them all.

"You know, my child, if you don't wish to give the gossips fodder, you must learn to control your display of emotions," said the irrepressible Miss Fairchild.

"I beg your pardon," said Rhian, at a loss.

"First of all, that dreadful gossip Lord Hampton told Mr. Carstairs that you, a spinster, had asked permission to waltz, and he has spread it throughout the assembly."

"I fail to see what is so amusing about that," said Rhian. "I have never danced the waltz before, at least, not in company, so I naturally thought—"

"Nevertheless, you and Jonathan should have known better than to say anything in front of such an infamous talebearer. But don't worry, I managed to turn the tables on him."

Rhian leaned closer and said, "Oh, do tell."

"I just reminded the person who told me about your odd request that Carstairs should have been as proper before he led out Miss Dalrumple and ruined her two seasons ago. Not to mention Miss Thornton the year before. Carstairs has managed to make a career out of disgracing young ladies."

Rhian laughed with delight. "Thank you, Aunt Rosie. You've saved the day! And I shall try to be more circumspect."

"Excuse me, my lady, Miss Fairchild. I don't know if

you remember me . . ." said a rotund gentleman of some thirty years, bowing and creaking in front of them.

"Of course I do, Lord Chuffington," said Rhian.

"So kind, my lady. Might I have the next dance?"

"I . . . Why, yes. Of course," said Rhian, after being prodded in the ribs by Aunt Rosie. She rose and took his arm, throwing a look of pure astonishment at the older lady.

Jonathan returned, balancing three glasses. He looked around before spying Rhian lining up for the country reel.

"What the deuce!" he muttered.

"My glass, Jonathan?" said Aunt Rosie, grinning knowingly at his scowl.

He handed her a glass and sat down by her side, continuing to glare in the direction of the dancers.

"Damned cheek," he grumbled as Rhian passed close by and smiled at him.

"Who? You can't possibly mean Lady Rhian!" exclaimed Aunt Rosie in strangled accents.

Jonathan failed to recognize the humor she saw in the situation and said coldly, "Of course not! I mean that gelding dancing with her."

"My, my! Such language!"

"Beg pardon," he growled automatically. "But why the deuce did she stand up with the fellow?"

"He asked; she said yes. It is what one does at a ball. Besides, Jonathan, I thought Lord Chuffington was a friend of yours."

"Chuffy's well enough on the hunting field or taking a hand at cards, but this . . . I don't like it," he said simply.

"I did warn you, my dear boy. The butterfly is just learning to fly. You should have expected it."

"Miss Fairchild?" said an aging gentleman in military

uniform. Aunt Rosie turned her back on Jonathan and proceeded to flirt outrageously.

Jonathan downed the contents of one of the glasses he held then looked down in disgust. Orangeate! Egads! What a depressing evening! I would have been better off going to that cursed literary salon with Pockets, he thought sourly.

By the time the music ended and Rhian had returned to him, he had decided to treat her coldly. Unfortunately, his behavior came across as petulant, so when a Mr. Seward asked her to dance, Rhian gladly accepted. And so it went for the next three hours.

Sitting down after yet another waltz with yet another partner, her head pounding unmercifully, Rhian said, "Aunt Rosie, I should like to go home. It is stuffy in here, and I have the headache."

Miss Fairchild looked from Rhian's creased brow to Jonathan's crossed-arm stance against a nearby pillar. "Of course, my dear. Jonathan!" she said, beckoning to him. He returned to their side promptly, forcing himself not to look at Rhian. "Jonathan, Lady Rhian wishes to go home. I'm going to remain here with the colonel."

"But, Aunt Rosie . . ." they said in chorus.

"I'm certain you can manage to get Lady Rhian home safely, my boy. Now, run along, do."

Dismissed so summarily, they took their bewildered selves to the door, waiting in silence until the carriage had arrived and they were seated inside.

"My lady," began Jonathan after the silence became uncomfortable. "I'm afraid we may have been precipitate in our actions."

"Precipitate?" said Rhian, her voice showing the dismay her countenance denied.

"Yes, that is, I realize you are not in the habit of attending balls such as this evening . . ."

"Rubbish!" she declared, rounding on him. "I have been attending Almack's regularly for the past six years. That I have chosen not to dance is neither here nor there."

"Chosen? Been unasked, more like!"

He caught the hand aiming for his face effortlessly. He pulled her closer, his dark eyes mirroring the anger in hers.

And the hurt, he realized abruptly. Without warning, he pulled her onto his lap and encircled her with strong arms. Rhian knew she should struggle, but his touch ignited fires deep within, and she clung to him hungrily, her lips seeking his, her hands kneading his broad shoulders.

With a breathless frenzy, she arched against him. His hand caressed her breast, and Rhian moaned, pressing closer, trapping his hand between their bodies.

The motion of the carriage stopped; the gas street lamps shone into the vehicle, and Jonathan removed his hand, gently easing Rhian back onto the velvet squabs.

"You should go in," he said hoarsely.

"You come, too," said Rhian urgently.

Jonathan hesitated, then shook his head. Not only did his present physical state make descending into the light inadvisable, but he couldn't trust himself to withstand Rhian's charms. With what he considered Herculean strength, he said, "No, I don't dare, my love. Tomorrow, we'll be together again. I'll call at two o'clock."

Reluctantly, Rhian nodded, and Jonathan helped her down, kissing each gloved hand before releasing her. He watched until she had disappeared inside; then, taking a deep breath, he ordered the driver to move over.

There were several near accidents and a great deal of

swearing as the lumbering carriage took flight through the streets of London and onto the North Road.

Rhian's cocoon of euphoria lasted until Fanny had prepared her for bed and curtseyed her way out. Rhian hugged the covers to her and snuggled down in bed. Enjoying the memory of Jonathan's embrace, she had no intention of going to sleep yet. She savored the deliciousness of his touches and his kisses until the prickles of doubt began to weigh heavily on her mind.

"Precipitate?" she said to the enveloping darkness.

She snuggled again, then frowned. Sitting up, she found the tinderbox and lighted the bedside candle.

"Now, what did he mean by that?" she asked herself.

She climbed out of bed and went to the dressing table to stare at herself ambiguously. She was not a green girl; she had seen a great deal of Society, although, up to this point, she had always been an observer rather than a participant. It was difficult to divorce herself from this situation and make sense out of Jonathan's enigmatic word—"precipitate."

But you must be dispassionate, she told herself sternly. Why would a man make a comment like that and then pull her into his arms?

Why, he had practically—here, she allowed herself the benefit of the doubt and placed the blame firmly on his shoulders—compromised her! What was he about?

What were his intentions?

Rhian started for the door. Then she stopped. Where was she going? There was no one in the household whom she could turn to for advice. Her father—that was unthinkable!

Tomorrow, she would go to Penelope's house and ask her brother-in-law for a man's opinion. But what could her sister's husband know about the mind of a gentleman like Jonathan, a gentleman of haut ton? Phillip was a decent man, but not very worldly.

Rhian paced back and forth across the room before flopping onto the bed again. This time, however, there was no hugging of memories. With single-minded determination, she decided to ask Lord Pembroke himself exactly what he had meant by "precipitate." And by his lovemaking.

Two more gowns had arrived, one suitable for receiving morning calls. It was a soft blue crepe, the lines graceful and alluring on her willowy figure. She knew she looked her best, but her expression was not soft; it was militant.

She sat in the shabby drawing room, stabbing at a piece of needlework she had been "working on" for six years. It was a hideous chair cushion Penelope had given her on the occasion of her first come-out so that she might be seen engaged in a feminine occupation when entertaining guests. Rhian hated it.

"My lady, a gentleman has—" said Tipton formally.

"Send him in," interrupted Rhian.

"Very good, my lady." Tipton returned momentarily and announced, "Lord Chuffington, my lady."

Rhian looked up in surprise before pasting a smile on her face and welcoming her unexpected caller.

"I'm so happy to find you at home, Lady Rhian," said the round Lord Chuffington, puffing slightly as he settled into the chair indicated.

"So good of you to call," said Rhian, automatically dredging up the polite inanities required by the situation.

"I just wanted to tell you how much I enjoyed your company last night at Almack's. I do hope you intend to frequent its renowned gatherings on a regular basis."

"I shall try," said Rhian properly. The fact that she had been a regular visitor to Almack's for a number of years had apparently escaped Lord Chuffington. It made her feel a bit chagrined that, until her waltz with Jonathan last night, her presence had gone completely unremarked. She comforted herself with the thought that her voice had been heard anonymously through her Quidnunc column.

"Lady Cowper, my lady, and her nephew, Mr. Seward," said Tipton regally.

Rhian's surprise showed plainly on her face as she greeted the patroness. Mr. Seward bowed deeply to her and settled himself near the fireplace, leaning against it with what was meant to be, Rhian felt certain, an interestingly masculine pose.

"Did you enjoy yourself last night, my lady?" asked Lady Cowper.

"Very much, thank you, my lady," lied Rhian, recalling how unpleasant Jonathan had made the evening.

Conversation continued in this polite vein for another ten minutes. Then Tipton entered again.

"Lord Sheffield and his sister, Lady Marion, and Mr. Reynolds, my lady," said Tipton.

Rhian hoped that these last additions would be all; Tipton would surely bust out of his coat with pride if any further luminaries turned up. And where, she wondered, would she put anyone else? Both ends of the mantel supported masculine elbows, all the chairs were taken, and she and Lady Cowper occupied the sofa.

"Lord Pembroke and Mr. Sims, my lady," announced

Tipton, his stentorian voice faltering as he surveyed the gathering.

Jonathan and Pockets found themselves standing in the middle of a crowded room, rather like the horses in the center ring at Tattersall's, thought Jonathan grimly. What the deuce were all these people doing there? He wished he'd stayed in bed. After driving until almost dawn, the last thing he wanted was to do the polite to a bunch of . . .

"My dear girl!" came a booming voice before either Jonathan or Pockets could speak. "Why didn't you tell me we were entertaining this morning?" Lord Ainsley made his way around the room, slapping backs and bowing deeply, oblivious to the stares of disapproval his crumpled evening clothes was occasioning.

Lady Cowper was the first to excuse herself. The remainder of the company scattered as well, and Lord Ainsley, bereft of feminine callers, found his way out the door, also.

He closed it, leaving Rhian alone with Jonathan and Pockets. Pockets cleared his throat nervously, sat down in a chair by the window, pulled out his poetry notebook, and lost himself in his compositions.

"How are you today?" asked Jonathan, taking the vacant spot on the sofa beside Rhian.

"I'm fine," she replied, not sure, suddenly, if she should go on the attack or not. Perhaps, in her naivete, she had misread everything. True, she reported on the idiosyncrasies of society, but how men and women behaved when they were alone was knowledge beyond her ken.

"Good." Jonathan felt unaccountably tongue-tied. He hadn't expected such reserve, not after what had passed in the carriage. "You had a great number of visitors today, I see."

"Yes. They called to . . . that is, I don't really know why they called. It was to welcome me—even though I have been a part of it—to Society. It is all rather disconcerting."

"My lady, another caller," said Tipton.

"Tell them I'm not at home," she said sharply. Then she eyed Pockets narrowly. "Mr. Sims?"

"Hmm?" said Pockets, looking up from his scribbling.

"I know it is frightfully forward and undoubtedly rude of me, but would you mind very much going away?"

Pockets, mindful of the warnings his aunt had pressed upon him about attending to the proprieties where Lady Rhian was concerned, frowned mightily.

"Don't think I really should, my lady. I hate to be disobliging."

"Oh do go away, Pockets. Lady Rhian is quite safe with me," said Jonathan.

"Ah, but is her reputation?" he asked with rare insight.

"Devil take you, Pockets!" exclaimed Jonathan.

"Please, Mr. Sims, you may leave us. Simply leave the door open; that will be quite proper."

Pockets looked dubious, but he glanced at the eloquent poem he had been composing and acquiesced. "Very well, but don't tell my Aunt Rosie. She'll be very put out with me."

"We promise," said Jonathan.

Pockets bowed over Rhian's hand and left. Jonathan sidled closer. Rhian stood up and moved to the window that overlooked the street.

"Something amiss?" he asked, his voice amused.

"Precipitate," she said, turning to confront him with the face of an accusing prosecutor.

"Preci . . . Oh, now I remember. Is that what has you

all in a dither?" Jonathan stood up and closed the gap between them in three strides. He touched her arm, and Rhian pulled away.

"What, my lord, did you mean by that?"

"Mean?" echoed Jonathan, his aggravation growing. "I meant, after watching you dance with every Tom, Dick, and Harry at Almack's, that perhaps I had been too precipitate in my attachment to you. Perhaps you were not as steady as I had led myself to believe."

Rhian's eyes blazed with indignation. "Perhaps, my lord, if you had not sulked all evening like a schoolboy, I would have been dancing with you!"

"I saw no indication of that, my lady!" he returned, his anger matching hers.

"How would you know? You never said a word to me after we waltzed."

"I never had the chance. And, if you'll recall, you didn't seem interested in conversation in the carriage on the ride home."

It was too much, and Rhian lifted her chin in a defiant dismissal. "Good day, my lord."

He started past her. He intended to leave and never darken her door again. It would serve her right!

But the tilt of that head, the red curls framing that flushed face . . . Jonathan took her hand in his and swallowed his pride. Surprisingly, it did not taste at all bitter.

"Rhian, I'm sorry. Please forgive me."

Her heart in her eyes, she turned her face to his and lifted her lips for a kiss. This time, there was no frenzy, just an infinite tenderness as his lips caressed hers. Their embrace brought them comfort, and they moved as one to the sofa again.

"We must watch our tempers," whispered Jonathan. "I don't want to lose you."

Rhian nodded, burying her face in his coat, ruining his cravat. But Jonathan knew he had never been happier. All the hopes he had ever had he now held in his arms. He wouldn't let anything come between them again.

Six

Rhian hurried into the bedroom, throwing off the old black gown as quickly as Fanny could unfasten and unhook her.

"I will never be ready in time," she said.

"It's fashionable for a lady to be late," said Fanny.

"But I don't want to miss any of the play!" exclaimed Rhian. She couldn't explain to the maid that the theater was the one place she had not dared venture on her own. Without an escort or the funds to purchase a private box, it had been impossible for her to attend the theater. And it was one of the few entertainments she had enjoyed as a debutante.

She was dressed in a gown which had been restyled from her second Season. It was a cream-color which had sported a profusion of blond lace and dozens of bows on the bodice and flounce. Fanny had carefully removed all of these furbelows and added a dark green ribbon at the high waist and a narrow row of the same ribbon to each sleeve and the neckline. On top of this ribbon, Fanny had painstakingly sewn tiny silk roses she had fashioned from more cream-colored ribbon. Another silk rose had been attached to yet another piece of green ribbon, and this was tied around Rhian's neck. The effect was fresh and simple.

She heard the carriage pull up in the street as she was slipping her feet into kid slippers. Pulling on her gloves, she allowed Fanny one final pat to her curls, pinched her cheeks for color, and hurried down the stairs.

They were assembled in the drawing room, all looking quite elegant. Rhian, though she knew her ensemble looked fetching, felt positively rural in her old gown. But one glimpse at Jonathan's admiring eyes made her doubts fly away.

"I'm sorry to keep you waiting," she said.

"We have only just arrived, my dear. Think nothing of it. I was a bit slow getting on my way, but such is the case when one gets older," said Aunt Rosie with her bull-dog smile.

"Older? You're younger than all of us!" scoffed Pockets.

"Well, I am certainly gayer than you and Jonathan, always writing this or reading that," she replied. "But we should be going; I do so hate to be seated after the curtain rises."

"I agree," said Rhian, allowing Jonathan to help her adjust her Norwich shawl. "But I think most of the patrons care only about being seen. They hardly pay attention to what is happening on stage."

"True, but arriving early, one can do both," said Aunt Rosie wisely, leading the way to the carriage.

Much to Rhian's delight, in the theater they had a box near the stage. She and Aunt Rosie sat in front with Jonathan and Pockets just behind them. Rhian found it more difficult than she had thought to concentrate on the play knowing Jonathan's knees were practically touching the back of her chair.

The curtain rose, and she was able to lose herself in

the performance. Edmund Kean, as everyone had said, was superb; his rendition of Shylock was so emotional, Rhian could almost forget Jonathan's proximity.

Then he leaned over her shoulder and whispered in her ear, "Magnificent, isn't he? Are you enjoying yourself?"

His warm breath sent a chill through her body, and Jonathan caressed her arm. His action made her flush uncomfortably, and Rhian found it impossible to return her full attention to the stage.

When the intermission arrived, she welcomed the cold champagne that was served. Friends of Jonathan and Pockets made their way to the box, including Lord Chuffington, much to Jonathan's displeasure. But this time he had nothing to quibble about; when anyone addressed Rhian, she would drag her eyes away from Jonathan with conspicuous reluctance. Then the curtain was going up again, and their visitors vacated the box.

Jonathan moved closer to Rhian, his hand resting on the back of her chair. At the end, Rhian's enthusiastic applause joined with everyone else's, but she couldn't have said if the performances were excellent or not. All she knew was that she was exhausted, her thoughts riotous still from Jonathan's light caresses as he whispered in her ear.

In the carriage once again, Aunt Rosie asked, "Did you enjoy the theater as much as you expected, Rhian?"

"Yes, it was very, uh, stimulating," she said, causing Jonathan to swallow a chuckle.

"Good! And now to Grillon's. I adore the place, you know, and it's been almost a year since I was there. I warn you, I intend to eat my weight tonight, my boys."

"That shouldn't destroy my purse," said Jonathan.

The hotel enjoyed the patronage of the *creme de la*

creme of British society, so, despite the advanced hour, it was crowded. They were seated to one side of the large dining room, in a position that allowed Aunt Rosie to observe and comment on every new arrival.

"Don't look now, but there is Hampton. He is trying to catch our eye, but we won't see him. Such a bore!" pronounced Aunt Rosie. "Oh, now here is that charming Lord Chuffington. Should I call him over?" she asked, a wicked smile directed toward Jonathan.

"I don't think so, Aunt Rosie, since I would have to throttle the man for ogling Rhian. And that, I am convinced, would ruin the evening for you."

"Hmm, probably, but here he comes anyway." She put on a frigid smile—not difficult for one with her forbidding features—and greeted the oblivious young peer. "Lord Chuffington, how good of you stop by, again, to greet us. But we mustn't keep you from your party."

"Why, no, I mean, thank you," stammered Chuffington, wondering how he had been outmaneuvered so neatly.

"Good evening," said Rhian, holding out her hand to dismiss him.

With a creaking of corsets, he bowed over her hand, kissing it lightly. "Good evening, ladies, gentlemen," he said, muttering to himself as he walked away.

"Damned cheek!" mumbled Jonathan.

Rhian looked puzzled; Aunt Rosie and Pockets shared a quiet laugh.

"You must forgive Jonathan, my dear. He is so primordial at times."

"Thank you for your opinion, Aunt Rosie," he said, raising one brow in a manner that would have intimidated a lesser soul. But Aunt Rosie just giggled.

They ate turtle soup, followed by a filet of fish served

with a delicate sauce. Then came the main entree, a tender roast lamb, some veal cutlets, and several vegetables. Champagne was the beverage, being the favorite of Aunt Rosie. A raspberry trifle with fresh cream was dessert, and was served with rich, steaming coffee.

If only they had hurried a little bit, thought Rhian dismally, as she watched her father leave his group of friends and weave his way across the room toward their table. But escape was impossible, and she pasted her usual smile on her face.

"Hello, Papa," she said.

"Wha . . . ? Oh, hello, my dear. Miss Fairchild, so good to see you again," said Lord Ainsley, exerting himself to bow before Aunt Rosie.

The exercise must have made his head reel because he grasped the table as he straightened up. With a crash, he sat down heavily on the plush carpeting, looking up in surprise as the cloth came off the table, sending the glassware and remaining plates cascading onto his lap. Aunt Rosie leapt to her feet and out of the way, but Rhian was not as quick, and the remainder of her trifle landed in her lap, followed by a cold bath of champagne.

"Papa!" she squealed, as Jonathan tried to wipe the gooey mess off her gown. She pushed his hands away and hurried to the door.

Jonathan motioned to Pockets to follow, and Aunt Rosie hurried after him. Jonathan helped the befuddled Ainsley to his feet, paid his shot, and rushed out the door also. Lady Holcomb, clucking sympathetically, guided Ainsley to her table.

Jonathan expected to be met with tears, or at the very least, angry ranting and raving. Instead, as he climbed into

Aunt Rosie's carriage, he was nonplussed to find the other three occupants in hysterics.

"Served the old blackguard right!" Aunt Rosie was saying. "Why, he might even sober up over that one!"

"I doubt it!" said Rhian. "If falling into that pond with Lady Holcomb didn't change him to a teetotaler, nothing will!"

"I do wish I had seen that!" declared Aunt Rosie. "Still, to have been privileged to witness tonight's debacle was wonderful! I shall dine out on it for the rest of the Season!"

"Say what you will, Lady Holcomb is a loyal soul," said Jonathan. "When I was leaving, she was dusting him off and taking him under her wing!"

"She wants a new husband," said Aunt Rosie, causing Rhian to gasp. "Didn't you know? She's been ousted from her estate by her son's new wife, and rumor has it, the new Lady Holcomb is increasing now. She wants the dowager out of their townhouse by next Season so she can return to town."

"I had no idea," said Rhian more soberly. Then the corners of her mouth curved wickedly, and she added, "She'll have quite a shock when she discovers Papa hasn't so much as a penny. There is the estate, a rundown shell of a house, but it is entailed and can't be sold. And the townhouse is mine."

"Yours?" asked Pockets, shocked at such an unusual state of affairs.

"It was my grandfather's; he left it to me. Papa is welcome to live there, but I don't fancy sharing it with Lady Holcomb."

"Perhaps someone had better just drop a hint in Lady

Holcomb's ear," said Jonathan, looking pointedly at Aunt Rosie.

This lady rubbed her hands together and said, "I would be delighted! Absolutely delighted!"

They had reached Rhian's house, and she invited them inside for tea, but Aunt Rosie was suddenly too tired and declined. Jonathan made as if to accept, but Aunt Rosie held him back and whispered, "Not at all proper, my boy."

So he declined as well, and, disappointed but happy, Rhian went inside.

"My lady! What happened?" asked Tipton, unable to manage his usual aplomb.

"What? Oh, this. Yes, I'm afraid I have ruined this gown. And Fanny worked so hard on it."

"But my lady?"

"It was just an accident; don't worry about it." With this, Rhian floated up the stairs. At the landing, she turned and called down, "Papa may look the same when he comes home, Tippy. You'd better warn Howard."

When Rhian was tucked up in bed, full of rich food and sleepy with champagne, she allowed herself to reflect on the evening. The meal at Grillon's—except for the ending—had been very entertaining. But the theater was more memorable with Jonathan's touch firing up her senses until she had been oblivious to everything around her.

The tiny, feathery strokes he had bestowed on her back, her shoulders, her arms, had kept her in a constant state of anticipation. It was as if she had contracted a fever, but it was not unpleasant in the least. Lying in her big bed, she wished she could hold him. She marvelled that the thought did not make her blush.

When she had been away at school, many years ago, she recalled whispered confidences with the other girls.

They had twisted rumors and half-truths together to form a sort of bizarre impression of what it would be like to be held and kissed by a man. Their clandestine discussions would lead to giggles covered hastily by their pillows, and blushes hidden by the darkness.

But nothing had prepared Rhian for the raw hunger she felt when she was with Jonathan. She wanted everyone else to vanish so they could be alone, so he could hold her and kiss her. The thought made sleep impossible, and Rhian climbed out of bed and lit a candle on the desk to work on her column. Finally, weariness allowed her to return to bed and sleep, her dreams fulfilling her desires until reality could.

"My Lady," said a voice, bringing Rhian awake with a groan. "My lady, Mr. Tipton said to tell you there was a man below asking for your father."

"Then why wake me?" she mumbled, turning over. The room was cold compared to her dream, and she only wished to pull the coverlet over her head and continue to bask in Jonathan's embrace. But the maid was insistent.

"It's not a gentleman, my lady. It's some man," said Fanny, managing to wrest the covers from her grasp and leave her open to the chill of reality.

But Rhian was awake now—grumbling, but awake. "What sort of man?"

"Mr. Tipton said something about a cent per cent."

Now she had Rhian's attention. "Where is my father?"

"He didn't come home last night, my lady," said Fanny, holding out a navy morning gown for Rhian to slip into.

Rhian's head came through the neck, and she said, "Thank heavens for that! Where is Tipton?"

"He's keeping an eye on him."

"Then ask Howard to tell Tipton I'll be down shortly."

"Yes, my lady."

Rhian dragged a comb through her red curls and twisted them into a severe chignon at the nape of her neck. She searched out her spectacles and placed them low on her nose. The reflection staring back at her was quite formidable, and she grunted in satisfaction before making her way down the stairs.

"Lady Rhian," intoned Tipton as she entered the study.

The man wore a shiny black coat that had seen better days. He had a mustache and a full beard, making it appear that he had no mouth. But he had a voice, and a cockney accent so thick Rhian was hard put to understand him.

"Well, wot 'ave we 'ere?" he said, rubbing his hands together.

Rhian saw Tipton stiffen, but she didn't allow herself to react. Instead, she walked past him, ignoring the stifling mixture of stale tobacco and blue ruin, and took up her position behind her father's desk.

"What may I do for you, Mr . . . ?"

"Smith, m'lady. An' I came 'ere t'see yer father, not some fancy miss, beggin' yer pardon."

Rhian tilted her nose in the air and stared at him through her thick glasses. "I see," she said finally. "Well, Mr. Smith, my father is not at home today. If you wish to conclude your business, you must conclude it with me."

"Well, well," he said, studying her and the situation. "It's a matter of debts," he growled.

"Of course it is," said Rhian haughtily. "And since my father has no money, you had best deal with me. I do."

He chuckled. Then he laughed. Then he guffawed and sat down in the straight-backed chair, clutching his sides.

At last, he contained himself. Rhian continued to stare down her nose at him, and he shifted uncomfortably.

His voice gruff, he said, "It's like this. I buy I.O.U.'s from gentl'men. I 'ave got me mitts on quite a few with yer father's name on 'em. I've come t'collect me money."

"May I see them?"

He pulled a wad of papers out of his pockets and started to hand them over, then he drew back suspiciously. " 'Ere now, missy, Bob Smith is no fool. I 'and 'em over when I gets me money." He sat back smugly.

Rhian raised her brows and pursed her lips. Then she said, "Surely, Mr. Smith, you don't expect me to pay for something when I haven't even determined if it is truly my father's signature. I'm not so green as that. Do you think you are the first cent per center who has tried this?"

"I jes' wants wot's mine," he pouted.

"And you shall get it, but I must verify the documents first."

Grudgingly, he handed them over. Rhian knew they would be authentic, but she went through the motions of looking at each one, adding up the totals as she did so. Just over five thousand pounds! This was the worst ever! She had no idea how she could raise such an amount!

"I can see, Mr. Smith, that these were indeed signed by my father. Now, how much do you want?"

"Full payment," he said, his accent as plain as day. He sat back expectantly.

"Rubbish!"

"What!"

"You heard me, sir. You probably bought these for a tenth of their value. Surely you don't expect me to pay full price!"

"Oh, yes I do! Unless . . ." he paused and leaned toward her menacingly.

Rhian noticed that Howard had slipped into the room along with Tipton. No doubt Angus and Harry were waiting in the hall. Howard, a tall, muscular man, cleared his throat. Mr. Smith turned slightly and, seeing him, took out his handkerchief and mopped his brow.

Rhian prodded him, saying, "Unless?"

"That is, unless you want t' offer me somethin' else . . . somethin' less, that is."

"Why yes, Mr. Smith, that is what I had in mind. You have vowels here for five thousand two hundred and twenty pounds. I am prepared to give you a bank draft for three thousand five hundred."

"Bank draft? I deal in cash."

"Very well, then you will have to come back tomorrow. Of course, for my protection, I will have my solicitor and perhaps a Runner here to oversee the transaction."

"A Runner!" he exclaimed, standing up and almost knocking over the chair as he backed away.

"If that doesn't appeal to you, Mr. Smith, and you won't accept my check, I'm afraid I'm at a loss—"

"Well, as t' that, my lady, I think maybe a check would do the trick."

"Oh, I don't know. That is a great deal of money, and I can understand your not wanting—"

"Oh, but I do!"

Rhian took out a check and wrote swiftly. She blotted it and handed it to Mr. Smith who stepped forward and then back, keeping a respectful distance.

He glanced at the check and blustered, "Wot's this trick? It's fer only three thousand!"

Rhian leaned across the desk, her hand out. "Either

accept it or not, Mr. Smith. That is all you will get out of me. And I promise you, if you ever darken my door again, I will lodge a complaint against you with the Runners, and you will find it difficult to do any more business, anywhere!"

Mr. Smith puffed out his chest, opened his mouth, then snapped it closed. Putting his hat on his head, he left the room, grumbling about the money-hungry ways of the rich.

Rhian sank back in her chair, removed her spectacles, and rubbed her eyes.

"Breakfast is ready, my lady, if you'd like some," said Tipton, gazing at her in admiration and sympathy.

"Thank you, Tippy. That sounds wonderful! And Tipton, when my father does come home, if he's sober, I'd like to see him."

"Very good, my lady."

"Rhian, what's this all about?" asked Jonathan, frowning fiercely at her and waving a piece of paper under her nose.

"What?" she asked, taking the paper from his hand. It was from the modiste, informing his lordship that the dresses his "friend" had ordered had been cancelled. Rhian handed it back, saying, "Blast!"

Jonathan grinned. "Such language!"

"She had no right to write to you just because I decided against those gowns. It was my decision."

"But why did you cancel them? You seemed very excited at the time. And the gowns seemed quite reasonable compared to Aunt Rosie's modiste." Jonathan didn't want to embarrass her by revealing that he knew money was a factor for her, judging by the worn furnishings around the room, not to mention that she seemed to wear the same gowns rather frequently.

"Oh, I don't know. When I started thinking about it, I realized I didn't need that many gowns. I'm not a fashion plate, Jonathan. Clothes are not that important to me," she added defensively.

"That's fine, but I was hoping to see you in that blue one; I would be the envy of all the other gentlemen," he added, sitting down by her side and taking her hand in his.

Rhian threw him a mischievous grin. "All the other gentlemen were what upset you so at Almack's last week, if you'll remember."

"I'd rather not," he said dryly. "But I wish you would reconsider. If it is a matter of funds . . ."

Rhian blushed and looked at him haughtily. "It is not always a matter of money," she said, crossing her fingers in the folds of her gown. Her pride would not let her admit to him that money was always a factor, especially with a father such as hers. Moreover, she worked too hard for her money.

Jonathan decided quickly it would not be worth another row to contradict her, and he said, "If that is what you wish, my dear, then so be it."

"Thank you, it is," said Rhian, pleased with her easy victory.

"Now, are you ready to go for our ride?" asked Jonathan.

"Ride?" said Rhian, her eyes widening in dismay. "I thought you said a drive."

"Did I? Well, I meant a ride. You do ride, don't you?"

"I know how," she replied hesitantly.

"Good, then go change into your riding habit. I have two horses outside, and I don't like to keep them standing too long."

"I'm not a very . . . experienced rider, Jonathan. As a matter of fact, I've never had the opportunity to practice very much. I'm afraid you'll have a very dull time of it."

"I don't mind," he said doggedly. "Now, run along, my love."

Rhian climbed the stairs like a condemned man heading for the gallows. When she reached her room, she said glumly, "Fanny, I am going for a ride."

"A ride, my lady?" asked the surprised maid.

"Yes, his lordship insists we go for a ride. Do I still have my riding habit?" she asked hopefully.

"Yes, my lady," said Fanny, causing Rhian to make a face.

"It's been six years; maybe it won't fit," said Rhian.

Fanny produced the garment—a beautiful, soft wool habit in a pale yellow which Penelope had insisted she order. It would have been beautiful on a brunette, but it had turned her fair complexion a sallow shade and clashed with her dark red curls. She hated the habit almost as much as riding.

When she had put it on, she and Fanny stood side by side in the cheval glass, their expressions grim.

"It still fits, my lady," said Fanny doubtfully.

"Yes, but it is as hideous as ever. And it is a bit tight. Still, I might as well get it over with. Let's just hope I don't disgrace myself this time."

Fanny agreed, crossing herself for luck.

Jonathan stood up as she entered the salon. He covered his surprise and lied cheerfully, "You look wonderful."

Rhian made a *moue* and allowed him to escort her to

the waiting horses. The mare, wearing the requisite side-saddle, was prancing daintily. Rhian held back.

"She's very well-mannered, Rhian. She's just a little restive from being kept standing."

Rhian allowed him to throw her into the saddle where she clutched the reins heavily, causing the mare to dance away from the groom at her head. Jonathan swung up on his gelding and led the way. Rhian stayed close behind him, her face tense, her eyes darting from side to side.

They rode in silence, Jonathan pulling back and allowing her to catch up with him. He was wearing an insufferable grin which would have annoyed Rhian had she been capable of turning sideways to look at him. The houses were thinning before Rhian finally asked their destination.

"We are going on a picnic, my love. It is most scandalous of me, I know, but I want to be alone with you, and this seemed to be the best solution."

When she didn't respond to his jest, Jonathan pulled up and stopped her mare by putting his hands over hers. "If you don't wish to go, I can take you home."

"No, I don't want to go home, Jonathan, but I can't relax until I am off of this beast."

"Beast? Little Bit? She's the gentlest horse I know. I bought her for my niece who is only ten years old. Surely you aren't afraid of her!"

"Terrified!" she said with a nervous laugh.

"I'm sorry, Rhian, I didn't realize you were so frightened. You should have told me."

"If I had told you, you would have asked why. And that is a sore subject," said Rhian, laughing grimly at her own jest.

"I see," said Jonathan. "Then I shan't ask," he added, continuing on.

They reached their destination, a secluded green lawn that led down to a picturesque brook. Jonathan helped Rhian dismount and secured the horses.

"Now, let me see. Ah, there it is." He produced a large hamper which had been placed behind a large rock. Opening it, he took out a blanket and spread it on the ground for Rhian.

Then he joined her and began pulling out the contents of the basket—cold pheasant, light scones and jam, apples and peaches, and a bottle of wine. He handed Rhian a plate and poured the red wine.

"Good old Ivey," said Jonathan. "He owns an inn not far from here. He was my batman on the Peninsula; taught me everything I didn't know, which was considerable." Then he raised his glass and said, "To us."

Rhian drank deeply, a giddiness assailing her that had more to do with the company than with the wine. They spoke of childhood and dreams, disappointments and desires.

Having cleared away the remains of their luncheon, Jonathan settled back on his elbows and looked up at the sky. Rhian lay down on her side, overtaken by the headiness of his presence. Jonathan smiled at her.

But after a few minutes, he asked tentatively, "Why are you so afraid of riding?"

"I knew you would want to know," she accused. "And we were having such a lovely time."

"You don't have to tell me if you don't want to," he said, but his curiosity was evident.

Rhian sat up and said, "Oh, very well, when I was only five years old, my pony ran away with me."

Jonathan was silent for a minute. Then Rhian stole a glance at his face, his lips quivering with suppressed laughter.

"It wasn't funny to a five-year-old!" she exclaimed, her own voice shaky.

"I'm sure it wasn't, my love, but it sounds funny coming from a grown woman. Frightened by a little pony?"

"It was a big pony! And then there was the other time . . ." she added softly.

"What other time?" he managed to ask evenly.

"It was my second Season. I was riding in the park when a group of boys set off some firecrackers. My horse reared up, throwing me off. My foot was still in the stirrup, and I was dragged . . ."

Jonathan enveloped her in his arms and kissed her. After enjoying his efforts for a moment, Rhian pulled back and asked, "What was that for?"

"To apologize for making you ride all this way, and to congratulate you on your courage for doing so." He kissed the tip of her nose.

"I just didn't want to disappoint you."

"You could never disappoint me, Rhian."

This required several more kisses which they both participated in equally.

Finally, in a fit of honesty, Rhian confessed, "Besides, I wanted very much to be alone with you, too."

This earned her another kiss, and Jonathan rolled over, taking her with him until he lay on top of her. His kisses became more urgent, and Rhian forgot caution and pulled him down, their bodies molding into one. Their breathing ragged, Rhian pushed him away in surprise.

"We shouldn't—"

"I know, I know. . . . But you are so beautiful, so irresistible—" Her kisses silenced him, and he forgot all reason until his own desires brought him to the brink of losing all control.

This wouldn't do! he told himself, tearing himself away from her. He looked down at Rhian, her expression one of frustrated longing as she tried to pull him back down. Jonathan shook his head to clear it and stood up. He stalked down to the brook, wishing he could cool his passion by jumping in. But that would only alarm Rhian more than his lovemaking.

"Jonathan?"

He took a rigid hold on his self-control. "What, darling?"

"Are you angry with me?" asked the bewildered voice.

Jonathan, smiling again, turned to Rhian who had followed him. He put his arms around her lightly. He touched her forehead with his lips and shook his head.

"Not at all," he whispered. "I love you, too much, and I find it almost impossible to control my desire for you when we . . ."

"I'm sorry."

"It's not your fault. It's just the way things are for a man, in love with a woman. We should marry before I lose control completely."

"Marry?" said Rhian, her knees buckling and her stomach doing somersaults.

"I love you, Rhian. Will you marry me? I know I should ask your father's permission, but it is your answer that matters to me. Will you?"

Rhian threw her arms around his neck, kissing him, and mumbling "yes" against his lips.

Jonathan, mindful of his duty to guard her reputation, kissed her chastely and then released her, saying, "We should be getting back. Aunt Rosie will be coming to fetch us both for that blasted musicale before we know it, and I do want to speak to your father."

Seven

"Your father won't have any objections, will he?" asked Jonathan, unaccountably nervous all of a sudden.

Rhian laughed, took his hand, and led him up the steps of her town house. "I don't even know if he'll be home."

The door opened, and Tipton bowed. "Good afternoon, my lord, my lady."

"Hello, Tipton. Is my father at home?"

"Yes, my lady, but I believe he is indisposed."

"Indisposed?"

"Yes, my lady."

"Is he ill?"

"Not exactly, my lady. Perhaps you'd like for me to ascertain," said the butler cautiously.

"That won't be necessary. I'll go up myself," said Rhian. Tipton put a restraining hand on her sleeve. "What is it?" she asked, a feeling of dread descending on her.

"There is a, uh, person with him."

"A person? Well, he'll just have to excuse himself for a few minutes. Lord Pembroke wishes to speak to him." Rhian started up the stairs.

Tipton made a strangling sound, and Jonathan looked at him sharply. "What is it, man?"

"His lordship! He's not alone," said the distressed old man. "He has . . . someone with him."

"A woman?" asked Jonathan. At the butler's nod, he was up the stairs in a flash—but he was too late. He heard a shocked, "Papa!" followed by a feeble scream and then silence.

Jonathan knelt down beside her still form. "Damn it, man!" he barked at Ainsley. "And in your daughter's house!"

"Well, dash it, a man's got to take care of his needs!" said the drunken roue, staggering toward the door, naked to the world. Fanny, who had been alerted by Rhian's scream, hurried to her mistress's side and looked up, screamed, and fainted dead away as well.

"For God's sake, man, cover yourself!" snapped Jonathan. "Where is her room?" he demanded of the butler.

"Right this way, my lord," said Tipton.

"Here now, Pembroke! Can't allow you to enter my gal's boudoir," exclaimed Ainsley.

"Shaddup!" he said, slamming the door on the naked man before picking Rhian up and carrying her to her bed. "Have your footman tend to the maid."

"Yes, my lord," said Tipton, vanishing for a moment. Then the butler returned, hovering nearby, wetting a handkerchief and handing it to Jonathan, then continuing to wring his hands.

Jonathan sat beside Rhian, placed the wet cloth on her forehead, and rubbed her hands, at a loss for what else he could do.

Tipton paced back and forth, his wrinkled brow furrowed deeply. "I'm so sorry, my lord! I didn't want to blurt it out . . ."

"It might have been better if you had. I shudder to think what scene must have met her eyes!"

"Oh, my lord!" Stopping in his tracks, the frail servant moaned weakly.

"Courage, man; we can't have you swooning on us, too," said Jonathan bracingly. "Do you have any hartshorn around here? Or lavender water?"

"I'm sure Mrs. Gilbert has something. I'll be right back." Glad to have a purpose, he hurried away.

"Bring some brandy, too," called Jonathan, thinking of himself as well as Rhian and the butler.

Rhian's eyes fluttered open. She frowned and whispered, "What happened?"

"You fainted, my love."

"I never faint," she said, her voice a little stronger.

"Good, then we won't have a repeat performance. Do you remember why you fainted?" he asked cautiously.

He certainly didn't want her to swoon all over again. But he needn't have worried. Rhian shuddered and nodded, but she didn't faint. Recalling the sight of her father and some female thrashing around on the bed, she turned a bright red. Jonathan ignored her embarrassment.

"Feeling better?" he asked cheerfully.

Rhian nodded. "I'm sorry you had to be witness to such a scene, Jonathan. What you must think! I will understand completely if you wish to withdraw your offer," she added, praying he wouldn't want to.

Jonathan stood up and glared down at her fiercely. "Is that what you think of me? That I would be so callow, so craven as to allow a drunken man's folly to ruin our chance for happiness?"

Rhian raised up on one elbow. "I'm sorry, Jonathan! I only thought to save you . . ." Rhian's green eyes looked like emeralds as they filled with tears. Really! she thought.

Turning into a watering pot on top of swooning! What had become of her?

Jonathan sat down beside her and gathered her into his arms while she spent her tears. "Shh, shh," he whispered. "I'm not angry with you, and I have no intention of ending our betrothal. I hope I'm not so witless that I would cut off my nose to spite my face!"

When she quieted, he handed her a handkerchief and ordered her to blow her nose. The reddened eyes staring back at him looked irresistible, and he kissed each one in turn. Then he turned his attention to her pouting lips.

"Harrumph!" Tipton averted his eyes until they had separated. Then he ushered in a blushing Mrs. Gilbert who handed Jonathan all sorts of vials.

"This one is lavender water for bathing the temples," she explained. "Even though you've come around, my lady, I think it would be advisable." The housekeeper set about dampening yet another cloth. "You've had a nasty shock, and your nerves are still overset."

"Thank you, Mrs. Gilbert, but Lord Pembroke can see to that," said Rhian, taking the cloth and handing it to Jonathan.

"Oh!" exclaimed the housekeeper. "Well, can I get you anything else? A little—"

"Nothing, thank you. That will be all," said Rhian, her eyes never leaving Jonathan's.

"Did you bring up that brandy, Tipton?" asked Jonathan without turning around.

"Yes, my lord."

"Good. Pour two glasses, one very small, and take the rest down to the other servants. I daresay everyone could use a medicinal dose after all the excitement."

"Very good, my lord."

They heard a drunken melody from down the hall; Mrs. Gilbert gasped and covered her face at the bawdy lyrics.

"And shut the door as you leave," added Jonathan, causing Mrs. Gilbert to gasp again.

But they heard Tipton persuading her to leave, and then the door closed.

"I will never live this down, Jonathan," said Rhian, but her expression was amused rather than incensed.

"True, my darling, so we might as well make the best of it. If your reputation is in shreds, we should at least enjoy ourselves."

With this, he rolled onto the bed, pulling Rhian over until she straddled him. He put his hand in her hair and guided her lips down to his. He kissed her thoroughly, and she began to move against him with untutored passion. Jonathan matched her movements, establishing a rhythm which drove her to further heights of arousal. Knowing he had reached his own limits, Jonathan did his best to calm her, holding her tightly against his chest, his hands stroking her hair and back as she whimpered, pleading for further unknown pleasures.

"Not yet, my sweet, not yet."

Gradually, her ardor cooled and she sat up, causing Jonathan to groan with his own frustration. Rhian slipped off his chest and lay beside him, staring at the ceiling in silence.

After five minutes of this, Jonathan turned on his side and looked down at her, his dark eyes twinkling. Rhian reached up and smoothed a lock of black hair away from his forehead.

"What has you looking so serious?" he asked gently, his hand reaching out to fasten the buttons across her breasts. He had no idea when he had unfastened them.

Rhian rolled away and sat up on the opposite side of the bed. She continued his task, and Jonathan crawled across and drew her back down with him.

"Aren't you going to answer me?" he asked, smiling as she frowned at him.

Suddenly, Rhian buried her face against his broad chest. Her speech muffled, she began, "I was wondering . . ."

"Yes?" he prompted, when she didn't continue.

"When I opened Papa's door—for I thought he had said to enter—I saw . . ." She shuddered against him, and he patted her shoulders.

"You can tell me anything, Rhian. I'll answer your questions as best I can."

She nodded against him. "He and that . . . woman were both, well, naked, and Papa was . . . that is, his . . ." But Rhian found it impossible to describe the bizarre act she had seen.

"He was inside her?" said Jonathan, continuing to stroke her hair as she nodded again. "It is perfectly natural, my love. Although, in your case, it requires marriage."

Wide-eyed, Rhian lifted her frowning face and stared at him. "So when you and I marry . . . ?"

Jonathan nodded this time, and Rhian dove for the comfort of his hard chest while one small hand fluttered about his shoulder nervously.

Smiling, Jonathan kissed the top of her head. "It really isn't as difficult as it may seem. It can even be quite pleasant."

Rhian looked up after a moment, her head cocked to one side thoughtfully. "You mean, like we were a few minutes ago?"

"Yes, only better. I promise I shan't be groaning by the time we separate then," he said seriously.

Rhian smiled at him shyly and buried her head again, snuggling against him in a way that made Jonathan groan once more and wrap his arms more tightly around her.

"I think I'm quite looking forward to that part of marriage," she said finally.

There was a knock on the door.

Jonathan and Rhian vaulted to their feet, straightening, tugging, and smoothing until they nodded at each other to signify they were both presentable.

"Come in," called Rhian, now several feet away from the bed and Jonathan.

It was a relieved Tipton who announced, "You have visitors, my lady. It's Mr. and Mrs. Banyon."

"Thank you, Tipton. I'll be down in a moment. Please put them in the drawing room." The butler left, and Rhian turned back to Jonathan. "I suppose you should go, Jonathan. I don't think I can appear completely innocent in front of other people right now if you are anywhere in my vicinity."

"Nor could I," he agreed.

"I'll send Harold up to take you out the back way. The horses will have been taken to the stables by now anyway. He'll show you." She leaned against him for a brief, passionate kiss.

"Until tomorrow, my minx," he breathed.

Rhian checked her appearance in the large mirror in the hall before entering the drawing room. It was an elegant chamber, rarely used because the gold draperies and upholstery, despite their age, were so formal. But it would never do to slight her sister and brother-in-law by placing them in the common salon.

"Good evening," she said, smiling.

"Good evening, Rhian," came the two responses, one cold and one congenial.

"What brings you out this evening? Are you going to the theater?"

"No, we did that the other night. We are dining with friends."

"I see," said Rhian, wondering what reason her sister could have for calling at such an hour.

"As a matter of fact," began her brother-in-law after receiving an elbow in the ribs from his spouse, "we happened to see you at the theater."

"Oh? Why didn't you come by at intermission?"

"That should be obvious!" sniffed her sister.

Rhian frowned. "I don't see why, Penelope. I would have been only too happy to introduce you to my friends."

"Friends, eh? You're certainly moving in fast company these days, sister."

"Fast company? I wouldn't call Miss Fairchild 'fast.' She is a very kind lady and very good ton."

"Perhaps, but those two men! We saw how that Lord Pembroke was after you. I inquired about his identity after watching the way he mauled you; why, I was sure he had offered you carte blanche. It was disgraceful! Is that how you bring honor to the Ainsley name?"

Rhian stood up. Looking down her nose at her sister, she said coldly, "I would like for you to leave, Penelope."

"I'm not finished yet! It's as plain as day that your actions are going to disgrace our poor father! I've a good mind to tell him to send you home before you can bring further shame down on our heads!"

"My dear," protested her husband ineffectually. She only glared at him.

"Penelope, I doubt very seriously that my actions have anything to do with our family name being dragged in the mud," said Rhian, thinking of the scene still taking place in their father's bedroom. Still, she didn't want to reveal that particular truth. Somehow, Penelope would make that her fault, too.

"Papa must be so ashamed! And if Mama were alive—"

But that was as far as she got. Rhian's eyes blazed, and she leaned forward until their noses almost touched.

"Never," she hissed, "Never, talk about Mama to me. You weren't there. You didn't know how things really were. Papa—"

"Don't you dare say a word against Papa! That man has put up with so much from you with your hoydenish ways. The things he has told me!"

"Papa! Ha! Your saintly Papa is upstairs right now with a doxy in his bed, falling-down drunk, and singing lewd songs for all the world to hear! That is what your Papa is! He needs no help from me in bringing shame down upon our name; he manages very well on his own."

"You hateful girl!" screamed her sister. Then she clutched at her husband's arm and groaned, "Phillip! Take me out of here!"

"Of course, my dear," said the hen-pecked man. They disappeared, and Rhian collapsed on the sofa.

After a moment, Phillip Banyon stuck his head in the door again and asked sheepishly, "Do you need any help, Rhian, in getting this, uh, person to leave?"

She smiled kindly at him. He was really a good sort of man. Too bad his good nature was wasted on Penelope.

"Thank you, Phillip, but I'm sure Harold and Tipton can manage. I'll be fine."

"Oh, well, if you say so. Then, uh, good evening."
"Good evening, Phillip."

Exhaustion caused Rhian to sleep late the next morning.
She awoke with a splitting headache and grimaced at the
sound of heavy rain as it spattered against the window-
pane. Fanny came in with a cup of hot cocoa and stirred
up the fire in the grate. Soon, Rhian was warm inside and
out.

"I think I'll start the day with a bath, Fanny."

"Very good, my lady. Here's the morning mail, my
lady," said the maid, handing Rhian a silver salver. While
Fanny busied herself in the dressing room with the bath
and hot water, Rhian sorted through the envelopes. There
were invitations on stiff vellum for a wide variety of di-
versions. Rhian shook her head at the impressive list of
hostesses who had suddenly discovered her existence. She
wondered what they would say when they learned of the
betrothal of the plain Lady Rhian to the handsome and
wealthy Lord Pembroke. They would be green with envy,
she knew, and they would throw their barbs her way until
they had accepted the surprising liaison, or until some
better gossip came along.

While Rhian soaked away her headache, there was a
knock on the bedroom door. Fanny answered and returned,
her eyes bright with excitement.

"What is it, Fanny?" asked Rhian.

"Oh, miss, do come and see!" She held out a towel and
then helped Rhian into a wrapper.

Rhian entered the bedroom and her mouth dropped
open. The bed, the chair, and the desk were covered with
boxes and packages.

"What in the world?"

"They're from the modiste, my lady! From that French lady you go to, and some other one I don't recognize."

Rhian picked up a box and read the label. "Richardson's," she said, frowning. "But I only ordered one gown from there, and it was much too dear. What are all these . . ." Rhian snapped her fingers. "Aha!"

"What is it, my lady?" asked the maid anxiously.

"Jonathan!"

"Lord Pembroke, my lady? Oh, I don't think that's at all proper!" exclaimed the scandalized maid.

Rhian held up the blue ball gown which Jonathan had so admired. "He must have had them working around the clock," she murmured, rubbing the elegant cloth against her cheek.

"I'll tell Harold to take them back!"

"You'll do no such thing!" said Rhian.

"But, my lady—"

"Oh, Fanny, don't worry. Lord Pembroke and I . . ." But Rhian wasn't certain she should reveal the news of her betrothal yet. After all, until Jonathan spoke to her father, it wasn't official. Then again, she fully intended to do as she pleased, no matter what.

"That's what has me worried, my lady," muttered the maid.

Rhian smiled and explained, "What I mean is, Fanny, surely there is nothing improper if my betrothed wishes to give me a few gowns."

"Your betrothed!" squealed Fanny, hugging Rhian tightly. "Oh, beg pardon, my lady," she said, remembering herself.

"That's all right, Fanny. I feel just the same way."

"What did his lordship say? Your father, I mean."

"He doesn't know yet. Not since . . . Well, Lord Pembroke could hardly broach the topic last night! So mum's the word," said Rhian, finger to her lips.

"Right, my lady. In that case, let's see how you look in these things!"

The orgy of dressing and undressing, accompanied by sighs of pleasure lasted over an hour. Finally, only one box was left, and Rhian firmly rejected putting it on. But Fanny opened it and laughed heartily when she pulled out a forest-green riding habit, complete with hat and shiny black boots.

"I guess his lordship plans on riding with you more often, my lady."

"So it seems," said Rhian with a grimace. "It is very pretty, isn't it? If only one didn't have to ride a horse to enjoy wearing it. I wonder how I should like riding say, a cow or a tiger."

"I think I would prefer a horse to a tiger." Fanny finished putting away all the gowns and helped Rhian dress in her black bombazine. "I want you to know, my lady, we will all be very glad you've decided to wed Lord Pembroke. It's about time you had someone to look after you for a change."

"Thank you." Rhian smiled at her maid. She hadn't thought of marriage to Jonathan in that light. So far, all she had considered was that she could kiss him any time and any place that she wanted. Pursing her lips, she tried on the idea of Jonathan looking after her. It wasn't *unpleasant* precisely, but it did raise a few questions.

She hadn't told Jonathan about the newspaper she owned, much less that she was the editor. He would definitely be surprised to learn that she had been earning her own way for the past four years. She hadn't meant to deceive him; the subject simply hadn't come up. What would he think about it? Rhian pushed this question aside.

Would he want her to give it up? That would mean giving up her manner of earning money, and money meant independence to Rhian.

Was she ready for that?

But the thought of not having Jonathan to love was much more distressing than not having the newspaper, so Rhian smiled, confident that she had worked through the problem.

But she had avoided the one question that was the crux of the matter. How tolerant was Jonathan? She had always known that if the ton discovered her occupation, they would shun her. Would Jonathan shun her, too?

Rhian slipped out the back gate and into the waiting hackney.

"Good morning, my lady," said Possum, the driver. "Lovely day today, isn't it."

"It certainly is," said Rhian, smiling behind her veil.

"Any special plans for th' day, m' lady?"

"No, just the usual. Except that I must be home by four, so you had best come to fetch me at half past three."

"Very good, my lady," said the driver, tooling the coach into the street.

Walking toward the front door, Jonathan paused, watching the unfashionable vehicle leave the alley. It was probably nothing, but he would have a word with Tipton to make certain the back gates were secured.

Tipton opened the door, bowing slightly and allowing himself a smile for his mistress's betrothed. "Good morning, my lord. I'm afraid my lady has just gone out."

"Oh? I'm sorry to have missed her. Do you expect her home soon?"

"Oh, I couldn't say, my lord. She mentioned several errands she had to do, and then there was the shopping."

Jonathan grinned. Perhaps he had started something by having all those gowns made for her. Not to mention the matching gloves, shoes, and mysterious underthings the modiste had assured him each one required.

"Did she receive any deliveries this morning?" he asked.

"Yes, my lord. A great many boxes arrived. I sent them up to her straight away."

Jonathan's curiosity made him ask, "What was she wearing when she went out?"

"Wearing? I couldn't say, my lord. Was it important?"

"What? No, no. Is Lord Ainsley at home?" asked Jonathan, handing the butler his card with the corner neatly turned down to show he had called in person.

"I shall ascertain, my lord. If you'd care to wait in the salon?"

Jonathan didn't sit down, but went to stand by the window, his mind rehearsing once again what he wanted to say. He had little doubt that his suit would be accepted, but he was still nervous. He needn't have been.

"Don't say a word, Pembroke," groaned Lord Ainsley when he entered the room. He was wearing a loud brocade dressing gown. Thin, hairy legs extended from the tattered hem when he sat down cautiously in the softest chair. His feet sported dancing shoes. He held his head in his hands, eyes closed.

"My lord," said Harold, holding out a vile-looking concoction. Ainsley took it and, with a hideous expression, pinched his nose and drank it down. He belched loudly and then opened his bleary eyes.

"Now, what can I do for you?" he asked in gravelly tones, scratching himself.

"I'm glad to see you're feeling more the thing this morning," said Jonathan, unable to hide the sarcasm from his voice.

Ainsley looked perplexed and said, "When did we last see each other?"

"Last night. Upstairs. You had a visitor in your room."

Ainsley groaned again and dropped his head to his chest. "Now I remember. Ghastly stuff, blue ruin. I don't even remember where the girl came from. But damn! I had to do something when I left Lady Holcomb! What a harridan!"

"The girl?"

"No! Lady Holcomb! Seems someone put a flea in her ear about . . . But that's not what you're here for, is it?"

"No, sir. I want to speak to you about your daughter."

"Rhian?"

"Of course Rhian," snapped Jonathan, his nerves and patience sorely tried.

"Well, it could have been the other, but I didn't think you knew her. But that is neither here nor there. Rhian, eh? She's quite a girl, you know. Not in the usual style."

"No, not at all. But I want to marry her, and we would like to have your blessing, my lord."

"She doesn't have a dowry, you know."

Jonathan glowered at the older man and said proudly, "I don't need her dowry."

"Oh, I've no doubt about that, but you had to be told, just in case. Or if she has led you to believe there'll be a big inheritance someday—"

"Lord Ainsley, let us understand one another. I am marrying your daughter because I care for her. While you may find such an emotion impossible to fathom, I assure you it does exist. Now, have I your permission to wed Rhian?"

"Permission? Of a certainty! And my blessing, too! Now, about the settlements . . ."

Jonathan spent the next half an hour engaged in one of the most distasteful discussions he had ever endured. Lord Ainsley was the most unnatural parent he had ever encountered. He didn't recall too much about his own father, except that the sixth Viscount Pembroke had been very lordly, but his mother had been heartbroken when he was killed in a hunting accident, so he assumed his father had been a kind man.

But Rhian's father expressed only a cursory interest in the provisions for her pen money and any future grandchildren before turning to his real interest: himself. He asked for a quarterly allowance and the gift of Rhian's townhouse. Jonathan drew the line at the house, saying it was not his to bestow, but he agreed to give his future father-in-law a generous annuity on the condition that he didn't live with them. That, declared Ainsley, suited him down to the ground.

Afterwards, Jonathan headed straight for his club where he ordered a large brandy, downed it swiftly, and ordered another. This one he consumed much more slowly, but he was considerably subdued when Pockets discovered him an hour later.

"Morning," said Jonathan, with a relaxed smile.

"Good morning to you," replied Pockets, looking at the empty glass Jonathan was twirling around the table. "You were out very early this morning."

"Early? Devil a bit! I haven't even been to bed!"

"Hmm. Not like you, Jonathan. Working all night on that novel, were you? That bad novel?"

Jonathan nodded, staring off into space.

"Are you finished with it?"

"Almost! Just the last few touches and *voila!*"

"Voila, indeed. Jonathan, you do remember that it is supposed to be a bad, very bad novel, don't you?"

Jonathan nodded again, closing his eyes sleepily.

"I think we better get you home, old man. You need some sleep."

Pockets helped Jonathan to his feet, and they managed to get out the door before Jonathan passed out. Outside, he revived sufficiently to climb into a hackney, and they were soon back at Pockets's house.

Pockets helped Jonathan upstairs, watching as his valet removed the crumpled cravat and boots. Jonathan waved the servant away and climbed into bed.

"Jonathan, is this the novel?" asked Pockets, eyeing a stack of papers on the escritoire.

"That's it," mumbled Jonathan, turning over.

"Mind if I read it?" asked Pockets. When no answer came, he picked up the manuscript and settled into the closest chair.

Eight

Rhian worked until three o'clock finishing her reviews and the Quidnunc column. The maid brought in the tea tray, and her clerk looked in, his expression troubled.

"Join me, Geoffrey. I've finished everything; I'm ready for a bit of conversation. How is that lovelorn broadsheet coming?"

The earnest young man came in and sat down opposite the desk, but he declined the offered tea and biscuits.

"It's a bit of a problem, really, my lady. I can hardly get anything done during the day for all the people coming by with advertisements for it. All sorts of people: tradesmen and women, solicitors, even a rector, and some of the gentry. It's a regular Picadilly Circus all morning."

"I thought you gave a different address where they could send the notices."

"I did, but since we were the ones announcing it, everyone guessed it was going to our paper, so they come here instead, telling me their sad stories, hoping their notice will be given special consideration."

There was a knock on the door and the maid looked in and said, "A lady to see you, Mr. Geoffrey."

He rolled his eyes, saying, "Another one." He left the room, returning a moment later with a pained expression on his young features.

"This one claims she's just been jilted and must find a new husband before her father finds her."

"Do you think we should cancel our plans?"

He shook his head and said, "I don't see how we could now without causing a riot on our doorstep. But I don't want to be around when it comes out. Just think of all the applicants! If they show up on our doorstep, we can forget about putting out a newspaper."

"I see what you mean." Rhian walked to the window that overlooked the street. A smart looking carriage pulled up and an elegant older lady got out and hurried up the steps. A handkerchief placed over her nose, she looked up and down the street before entering. Rhian's eyes widened, and she hastily stepped back from the glass.

"Who is it?" asked Geoffrey over her shoulder.

"An acquaintance. Get rid of her as quickly as possible, Geoffrey."

"Of course," he said and hurried away.

Rhian went back to her desk, but she was too fidgety to accomplish anything. What on earth was Lady Holcomb doing here? she mused. Minutes passed and still Geoffrey could be heard talking to her father's admirer. If her father had let slip that she ran a newspaper, the cat was indeed set among the pigeons!

She heard another carriage come to a halt outside and looked out the window surreptitiously. It was her hackney cab, come to fetch her a few minutes early. He knew better than to come inside, but Rhian watched, in a panic, as he hailed Lady Holcomb's footman.

Rhian opened the window, putting her ear to the opening to try and hear their conversation. Then the door to the shop opened, and Lady Holcomb came down the steps, once again surveying the lay of the land. Rhian jumped back, closing her eyes as if this would prevent Lady Holcomb from seeing her.

She stayed hidden behind the curtain until she heard the carriage drive off. She peeked outside to be sure it was safe, then grabbed her coat and hat, adjusting the veil to cover her hair and face.

"What did she want?" asked Rhian as she passed Geoffrey.

"Just to leave an advertisement for the broadsheet. Seems she's just discovered her prospective husband is penniless, so she is in the market for someone new. See what I mean? An absolute circus!"

"I know, Geoffrey, but it won't last much longer, and we shan't do this again! In the meantime, engage another clerk and set up a desk nearer the door so he may deal with our visitors."

"Very good, my lady," grinned Geoffrey.

Rhian bid him a hasty good-bye and left.

Jonathan woke around six and went downstairs. He was ravenous and ordered tea in the library. Pockets was sitting at the desk reading; he looked up sharply at Jonathan's entrance.

"Good afternoon," said Jonathan, yawning and stretching. The butler entered with the heavily laden tea tray, and Pockets watched in silence as Jonathan filled a plate and poured a cup of tea.

"Would you like something?" he asked, swallowing a tart whole.

Pockets stood up and strolled over to the fireplace, leaning on the mantel without looking the least bit relaxed.

"What the devil were you about, Jonathan?" he asked

finally, running his hand through his hair in an exasperated manner.

Jonathan put down the scone he was holding and threw back, "What the devil are you talking about? Have you taken leave of your senses?"

"That's the question I should put to you!" He strode back to the desk and picked up the manuscript, dropping it with a loud thump!

"Who told you to read that, Pockets? It's not properly finished yet."

"It may not be finished, but it is quite proper, good and proper. As a matter of fact, it is one of the best, most properly written novels I have ever read! What the deuce were you thinking about? Didn't you even try to make it a bad one? What will it prove if everyone loves it? I'll tell you what! It will only prove the reading public has the sense to know a fantastic novel when they read one!"

"It's not that good!" exclaimed Jonathan, torn between pleasure and annoyance.

Pleasure won out when Pockets said grudgingly, "It's at least ten times better than mine, and I've been working and polishing for years! Damn it all, man, you've got real talent!"

"I thank you for the kind words, Pockets, but it still doesn't mean anyone else will like it."

"Believe me, they'll like it. The characters are well drawn, and the plot is beyond interesting, it's positively poignant. Of course, it's a thinly veiled story of your courtship with the Lady Rhian, but since you'll be publishing it anonymously, no one else will know that. By the way, congratulations on your betrothal."

"How did you know about that?"

"It's all in there," laughed Pockets, pointing to the manuscript.

"It was that obvious?"

"For me, yes, but then I watched your progress with it and with Lady Rhian. That's what really gave it all away. Other people, without knowing who authored it, wouldn't guess. Have you spoken to her father yet?"

"This morning. He's a conscienceless old reprobate. I don't see how Rhian has endured keeping him about all these years."

"It's what one does," said Pockets reasonably.

"I suppose, but I told him I won't have him living underfoot once we're married. He was quite acceptable of the idea once I agreed to settle an annuity on him."

"You're too generous, Jonathan."

"It was really just a bribe to get Rhian away from him. I told him I'd withdraw the funds if he lets her find out about it. I've sent an express to my mother in Bath; it wouldn't do for her to be the last to know. The notice should be in tomorrow's paper."

Pockets laughed. "Then you'll be well and truly caught in parson's mousetrap."

"Not a bad place to be," said Jonathan, grinning.

"Better you than I. But that still leaves us with the question: what are we going to do about the wager?"

"I suppose I can publish it and see if it's well received. Then we'll go from there."

"I tell you, Jonathan, you've got to write another one. Only this time, make sure it is truly atrocious," said Pockets.

"Or you could write it," teased Jonathan, earning himself a glare and a scone thrown at his head.

* * *

Wearing one of the new gowns Jonathan had ordered for her, Rhian felt equal to anything, even attending one of Mrs. Bingley's literary salons. She hadn't been to one since the night she and Jonathan met, and so much in her life had changed—her appearance, her outlook, even her *raison d'être*. She dreaded the inevitable questions.

But although Aunt Rosie had declined emphatically, Jonathan and Pockets would be there lending their support. Pockets was to read several of his poems that Rhian wanted to hear.

When she entered the salon, Jonathan greeted her with a chaste kiss on the cheek, mindful of Pockets who was absorbed reading over his poems.

"How are you this evening?"

"I'm fine, thank you. And you?"

"Very well," said Jonathan, smiling at the social niceties which still had to be observed despite their close relationship. "I spoke to your father this morning, and he approves."

Rhian's smile lighted the room for Jonathan, and he risked embarrassment by kissing her swiftly on the lips.

"Wish it could be more, but . . ." he whispered, cocking his head in the direction of the oblivious Pockets.

"Me, too," admitted Rhian, blushing at her boldness.

"I see you received your presents."

"Yes, but you shouldn't have, Jonathan. It really wasn't necessary," she said.

"Nonsense. I'm really just being selfish. I enjoy making you happy and love looking at you in pretty gowns, so you see, I was only thinking of myself."

"You are very gallant, but thank you."

"My pleasure. And I have opened accounts for you with both dressmakers. All the bills will be sent to me."

Rhian frowned and said quickly, "Jonathan, I can't allow that! I am quite able to pay my own bills!"

He frowned back at her, not giving an inch, his face like a stone. "Perhaps if it were only for you, but I happen to know you also pay your father's gambling debts."

With a gasp, Rhian said, "How do you know about that? Surely Tipton—"

"Of course not! Your man would go to the grave before revealing anything you didn't want him to! No, it was by accident, really. Chuffy's the man who sold your father's I.O.U.'s to that scoundrel. When he read about our betrothal, he confessed to me what he had done. He was drunk at the time, or he would never have done so at all. And he said if he'd guessed which way the wind was blowing, he would have come to me instead."

"That old school loyalty," muttered Rhian.

Jonathan grinned. "Yes, but it would have been much better for you if he had. I would have made short work of the man."

"In other words, you would have paid him off for me," said Rhian dryly.

"Exactly. You shouldn't have to deal with such riffraff!"

A glimmer of a smile appeared on Rhian's face, and she asked innocently, "So you would have handed over the five thousand?"

"Five! Your father plays deep!"

"Unfortunately," she said. "But you would have paid all of that for me?"

"Yes, but I probably could have gotten him to accept four," said Jonathan, giving her a condescending smile.

"I paid three thousand."

"Three?"

"Yes, three. And I also warned him that if he ever

showed his face at my door again, I would inform the Runners and the magistrate."

Jonathan's deep laugh caused Rhian to give him a pert smile. He swept her an elegant bow, saying, "I defer to your wisdom, my lady tigress. Should I ever get into trouble, I'll ask for your assistance, you may be sure." He glanced in Pockets's direction before giving her cheek a kiss. "Nevertheless," he said, taking her hand in his, "I want you to use the accounts I set up. We will very shortly be man and wife and everything I have will be yours, my love. Promise me?"

Rhian's eyes misted over, and she nodded solemnly. It was odd, she reflected, but it made her feel warm inside to know Jonathan would always be there to take care of her.

Jonathan patted her hand and turned saying, "Ready to go, Pockets?"

"What? Oh, yes, yes. I was just making sure everything was straight. I'm a little nervous," he admitted.

"I never would have guessed," said Jonathan, ushering Rhian out the door.

When they first arrived, they endured a brief grilling by Mrs. Bingley and then found chairs in the back row, which suited Jonathan very well. They listened to a young lady expound on the delicacy and beauty of nature for fifteen minutes before she finally finished. Pockets rolled his eyes and covered a yawn.

"When are you reading yours?" asked Jonathan.

"After refreshments," said Pockets.

"I'm looking forward to it, Mr. Sims. I have heard your work before," said Rhian.

"You mean *The Dastardly Duke?*" said Pockets, chagrined.

"No, I mean your poetry, and I was delighted to hear you were doing a reading tonight."

Jonathan, surprised by her interest, asked, "Why on earth do you want to hear Pockets read his bits and pieces?"

"Have you ever heard his poems?"

"Of course, now and then. But I didn't think they were that good," said Jonathan bluntly.

"Thank you," grumbled Pockets.

But Rhian ignored Jonathan and said enthusiastically, "Then you've not heard the ones about when he was a soldier. They are very engrossing, rather in the same vein as Coleridge's *Kubla Khan*."

"I didn't realize. All I've ever heard is some of his satire. It is rather good, and so I've told him," added Jonathan defensively.

Rhian chuckled quietly. "I don't doubt it, my dear. If you greeted all his efforts with the same appraisal that you accorded his *Dastardly Duke,* I daresay he would no longer number amongst your friends."

Jonathan flushed uncomfortably at the memory. Then he smiled and said, "But if I hadn't made such an oaf of myself, I would never have met you."

"True! I wouldn't have known you needed my help."

"Minx," he whispered in her ear.

"Oh, listen, Jonathan, someone is reading an excerpt from his novel. Do try to control yourself," she teased.

The young man finished and everyone applauded politely, including Rhian and her two escorts.

Rhian leaned forward and whispered, "I really don't know why anyone would read an excerpt. Even if the work is decent, it loses so much when taken out of context."

"So you like novels?" asked Pockets.

"Not particularly. Most of them are really very bad," said Rhian, causing Pockets to jab Jonathan in the ribs.

When refreshments were served, Pockets disappeared, saying something about getting ready. Jonathan went in search of refreshments, and Rhian was left on her own.

"My dear Lady Rhian! How are you? It's been much too long!" said Mrs. Bingley, speaking in gushing tones as was her usual habit.

"I'm fine, Mrs. Bingley," said Rhian.

"Of course you are," said the older woman with a knowing wink. "And I see you are here with Lord Pembroke."

"And Mr. Sims," added Rhian.

Mrs. Bingley waved her hand, dismissing Pockets's presence as of no importance. "We have managed to keep up with your whereabouts, of course, since you've been mentioned in several of the social columns lately. Your dear father must be so proud."

"I don't think finding one's name in a gossip column is necessarily an occasion for pride," said Rhian dryly, wishing she could think of some way to send this woman away.

"Are we to be listening for wedding bells?" asked Mrs. Bingley archly.

Rhian turned a frigid glare her way and said, "That, madam, is really none of your business."

"Oh, la, Lady Rhian! You mustn't take offense! We are, all of us, so delighted by your late blooming!"

Rhian turned red with anger, but Jonathan appeared and vanquished the irritating dragon with a simple, "Good evening, Mrs. Bingley. I believe Mr. Sims wishes to begin. We'll have to find our places." He sat down beside Rhian, neatly blocking Mrs. Bingley's entrance into the back row. She nodded haughtily and moved away.

"Thank you, Jonathan! What a dreadful busybody!"

"That's me," he quipped, "Jonathan the busybody slayer." He took her hand and squeezed it. Instead of letting it go, he held it in his lap, causing the turbaned lady at the far end of the row to puff up with indignation. Rhian shifted closer to Jonathan and smiled at the matron sweetly. It had the desired effect—the scandalized lady got up and moved to another location. Rhian grinned, wondered at her own temerity, and removed her hand from Jonathan's lap. She was not going to write about herself in the Quidnunc column, but for what she had just done, anyone else would have found themselves in print for all the world, all the ton, to see.

Pockets stood up and walked to the lectern. "Soldiers Eternal," he announced.

Jonathan suppressed a shudder, more in sympathy with his friend than ever before. "Takes courage," he whispered to Rhian. Rhian nodded, but was soon lost on the battlefield at Waterloo.

When Pockets read the last line, ". . . and to rally at the flag, at the grave, forever," there was hardly a dry eye in the salon.

Rhian sniffed, and accepted Jonathan's handkerchief. Jonathan, she noticed, was looking all around the room rather than directing his gaze at others in the emotional audience.

"See what I mean," she said, standing up and joining in the ovation Pockets had inspired.

Jonathan pumped Pockets's hand when he returned to his chair, saying sincerely, "Now that was a work of literature!"

Pockets blushed, smiling from ear to ear.

"Jonathan's right, Mr. Sims. You should look into having your work published."

"Do you really think it is that good?" he asked eagerly.

"I do," said Rhian.

"I wouldn't know how to go about it," he said, frowning slightly.

"Why don't you ask your aunt? She may have some knowledge about such things," said Rhian, thinking all the while that she would just drop a word in Aunt Rosie's ear about Penelope's publishing house. Maybe then she could make both Mr. Sims and her sister happy by writing a rave review of his poetry.

"Can we go now?" interrupted Jonathan. "Mrs. Bingley's niece is starting to warm up on the harp; I don't think I can bear sitting through another of her renditions."

"Me either!" agreed Pockets. "Let's say our farewells before we are trapped again."

When they returned to Rhian's house, they were surprised to find a sober Lord Ainsley waiting for them in the salon. Slapping Jonathan on the shoulder and winking at Pockets, he said heartily, "Just wanted to be the first to toast the happy couple!"

"Thank you, Papa," said Rhian, accepting a glass of French champagne.

When everyone had been served, Lord Ainsley lifted his glass and said, "To the happy couple!" He then drained his glass. The others took a sip.

Raising a replenished glass, Ainsley said, "To my future grandchildren!" He drained the contents again, ignoring Rhian's blush.

"To your health," said Pockets, hoping to steer the conversation toward safer topics.

Ainsley drained another and another, before remembering he was supposed to propose a toast first. "To both of you!" he said, his words slurring slightly.

Jonathan leaned over to Rhian and whispered, "I think Pockets and I better leave before he gets more—"

"May you have years and years of wedded beds—"

"That's very nice of you, Lord Ainsley, but we have to go. Good night, my dear."

"Good night, my lady," said Pockets, turning to Ainsley. But Rhian's father was already mumbling unintelligibly under his breath and turning the champagne bottle up to his mouth.

At the door, Jonathan put his arm around Rhian and gave her another kiss, this one much more compelling than the last.

"Jonathan," she whispered, holding him back. "Meet me in the garden in an hour; I'll unlatch the back gate."

He nodded and followed Pockets out the front door, his step jaunty, whistling a little tune.

Jonathan was early at the appointed rendezvous, but Rhian was just as eager and arrived only moments later. She unlocked the gate and flew into his arms.

Chuckling, Jonathan led her to a stone bench, hidden from both the house and the stables by the overgrown foliage.

"Is that why you asked me to come back?" he teased.

"Yes, it's very difficult being proper all evening when I am with you."

"I know exactly what you mean," he replied, slipping

his arms around her and kissing her thoroughly. He pulled back finally and said, "When do you want to have the wedding? At the end of the Season?"

"That's two months away!" she exclaimed.

"True, maybe we should make it around the first of June. Where?"

"At St. Paul's, I suppose."

"All right. And where do you want to go for our wedding trip? Europe? The Greek Isles?"

"I hadn't thought any further than the wedding, Jonathan," said Rhian, resting her head against his chest.

"Well, think on it now, my love. I've been to both, and I must say I think them vastly overrated. Now Switzerland might be nice, somewhere up in the Alps where it's cool and you'll need warming up."

Rhian grinned at his suggestive comment and said audaciously, "I don't think you need worry about that."

"You really are my green-eyed minx!" he laughed. "All right, if you have no strong preference, I'll surprise you." He returned to kissing her, and Rhian forgot all about wedding services and trips, lost in a hazy world of passion. At last, Jonathan set her away from him and declared his intention of leaving. Rhian protested, but he stood firm and let himself out by the garden gate, cautioning her to lock it after him.

Rhian went into the house, her spirits soaring. It was very late, almost dawn, and she knew she needed to sleep before going to work, but she found it impossible. When the sun had risen and the streets came to life, Rhian dressed and went to the office.

* * *

Rhian napped in the afternoon to get ready for her evening at the Fitzhugh's ball. She awoke with a fresh sense of excitement knowing she would waltz with Jonathan.

She dressed in another new gown, this one was a Persian blue with a silver overnet. She was about to put on her mother's pearls when Harold knocked on the door.

"This package just arrived for you, my lady."

"Thank you, Harold." Rhian took the package and tore off the paper. Inside was a long, narrow box of blue velvet. She opened it and expelled a soft, "Ooh!"

"What is it, my lady?" asked the excited maid.

"Look!" Rhian lifted a necklace made of intricate gold filigree encrusted with twinkling sapphires and diamonds.

"It's lovely," said the maid.

"Isn't it? Here, put it on me, Fanny."

"Ooh! My lady, you look beautiful!"

"Thank you, Fanny," said Rhian, subdued by the magnificence of the gift. She looked in the box and found one of Jonathan's calling cards. On the back, he had scribbled, *"Plus qu'hier, moins que demain."*

"What's it mean, my lady?"

"It is a French expression which means he loves me more than yesterday, but less than he will tomorrow." Her voice broke slightly and tears filled her eyes.

"He'll make you such a wonderful husband," said Fanny, swiping at her own misty eyes.

"Lord Pembroke has arrived," said Tipton from the open doorway.

"Thank you. Tippy. I'll be right there," said Rhian, scrambling to put on her slippers and patting her red hair one last time.

In the salon, Aunt Rosie presented her cheek for a kiss and remarked on Rhian's lovely jewelry.

Rhian smiled, saying, "It is a gift from Jonathan." She turned to him and held out her hands. Jonathan came forward and kissed her cheek.

"Not so much a gift, as a loan," said Aunt Rosie. "Unless I'm much mistaken, those are the Pembroke sapphires. I would have thought your mother had them."

Rhian looked at Jonathan in surprise.

"She did," he confessed. "But evidently, even in Bath, news of our whirlwind courtship had spread, and Mother had them cleaned up, waiting for the announcement of our betrothal. When I sent her word, she sent these back to me with her blessings."

"Oh, Jonathan, that makes me feel so much better!" said Rhian. "I was dreading meeting your mother. I was so afraid she wouldn't like me."

"Not like you?" asked Jonathan, incredulous.

"Rubbish!" said Aunt Rosie succinctly. "Of course she will like you! You're going to make her a grandmother!"

Rhian blushed, and Jonathan suggested quickly that they should be leaving.

The Fitzhugh's ball was an annual affair where only the best people were invited. The refreshments were legendary, from lobster to the most delicate pastries which their French chef prepared personally. No one in London, it was said, could match his touch, and he could not be bribed to reveal his secrets. They served only the best champagne, and it flowed copiously, helping to make the gathering a convivial one.

Rhian found that being a betrothed lady affected her dance card not one whit, except that her partners were more likely to be older or hardened bachelors who were definitely not hanging out for a wife. Jonathan, in a fit of masculine propriety allowed no one to waltz with her except himself and Pockets. This suited Rhian since she had no desire to be so very intimate with virtual strangers.

Unfortunately, she also discovered that her new status made her the target for more than a few jealous glances from newly come-out misses and their mamas. But this Rhian took in good part, knowing she was not losing friends but only rivals.

Jonathan took her in to supper, seating her at a table of young people, including Pockets and Aunt Rosie, who presided over their table like the queen mother. Rhian wanted very much to take out a paper and pen and record some of her more outrageous observations, but she didn't dare. Instead, she committed the very best to memory, hoping she would be able to recall them for her column.

Aunt Rosie was in her element, giving a scathing commentary on the older members of the gathering. One young man, who was in his cups, listened in indignation as Aunt Rosie related how his grandfather had wagered an entire estate on the turn of a card.

"And he lectured me only last month over my gambling losses!" exclaimed the young man.

Aunt Rosie wagged a finger under his nose and said, "But the difference is, young Windham, your grandfather won!"

This story caused one eager young lady to ask, "Do you know anything outrageous my aunt has done? She is forever prosing on about my behavior."

"And your aunt is?"

"Lady Holcomb," she said with a tipsy giggle.

Aunt Rosie pursed her lips as if trying to think of something. Then she shook her head and advised the young miss, "You would do well to listen to your aunt's advice, my dear. Including, I am certain, not to drink too much champagne. Mr. Stephens, why don't you take your sister back to your aunt?"

When Miss Stephens was seated beside her aunt again, Rhian smiled at Lady Holcomb, only to receive the cut direct. She looked around, amazed.

Aunt Rosie leaned closer and asked, "What was that about?"

"I have no idea. Perhaps she is still angry about my father," said Rhian, wondering privately if Lady Holcomb had seen her at the window of her office after all.

They started back to the ballroom and Jonathan, seeing Lady Holcomb pass by ignoring Rhian completely, asked, "What was that about?"

"I think she is taking out her anger at Papa on me," said Rhian, hating the fact that she could well be telling Jonathan a lie. But her suspicions were best kept to herself.

After supper there was another waltz, and Jonathan held Rhian close and scandalized all the old tabbies by whispering in her ear and making her blush prettily.

"And if we were alone," he breathed, "I would be doing much more than simply talking to you. I would be making love to you until dawn."

"Jonathan! Shh! Someone will hear!" she whispered.

"I couldn't care less," he said stoutly, but lowered his voice as he continued to tease her.

When Aunt Rosie finally declared the evening at an end, Rhian was radiantly exhausted. She whispered to Jonathan that she wanted to see him in the garden, but he reluctantly reminded her that she had an early fitting for her wedding gown and would need a good night's sleep.

Rhian was too tired to protest and when she finally arrived home, fell asleep as soon as Fanny blew out her candle.

The next fortnight passed as a dream for Rhian. She worked hard at the paper each morning and spent every other waking hour either with Jonathan or thinking about him. Aunt Rosie became her mentor, shopping for her trousseau and helping with plans for the wedding.

Aunt Rosie also insisted on throwing a ball to celebrate their betrothal. Rhian protested, saying one month until the wedding was hardly enough time to plan and hold an engagement ball. But when Aunt Rosie asked Rhian if she had ever had a ball thrown in her honor, Rhian had to admit that she had not.

"Then it's about time," said Aunt Rosie, brooking no further arguments.

They settled on the night of the fifteenth of May, Aunt Rosie suggesting they should have a Roman theme and call it the Ides of May Ball. But Jonathan vetoed this, saying he would tire too quickly of people teasing him to "Beware the Ides of May."

"I'm too happy about this," he declared stoutly, "for anyone to make light of it."

"Very well, my boy. Have it your way. Just leave everything to me! It will be a night to remember!"

So the plans were set for the ball and for the wedding breakfast, and they had posted the banns. They rushed headlong toward the engagement ball and the wedding.

Early one afternoon, as Rhian was returning from the paper, she was surprised when Tipton informed her that Lord Pembroke was waiting for her in the salon. Fortunately, she wore a simple lavender gown under her black cloak, so all she had to do was remove her black bonnet in order to be the elegant Lady Rhian once again.

"I wasn't expecting you, Jonathan," she said, presenting her cheek for a kiss.

Jonathan obliged her with a quick peck, but before she could protest, he said, "Rhian, I want you to meet my mother, Lady Margaret Pembroke. Mother, this is Lady Rhian Ainsley."

Rhian flushed a deep shade of scarlet and curtseyed to her future mother-in-law. Lady Margaret patted the seat beside her on the sofa and looked at Jonathan.

"You may leave now, Jonathan. Come back for me in twenty minutes."

"Mother . . ." he said with a warning in his voice.

"I shall behave, and I promise not to tell Rhian all your childhood secrets. Now, be a good boy and leave us alone."

Reluctantly, Jonathan did as he was bid.

"He is really a good boy, although there was a time when I despaired that he would ever settle down. He was so reckless in his youth."

"I thought he was a scholar," said Rhian.

"He was definitely that, but I think that made him all the more restless. He could never just be a normal little boy, playing with tin soldiers. He had to be organizing all the children in the village into a unit of trained soldiers. He was forever telling them to do something for someone. He was quite a little general, my Jonathan. But enough about him. Tell me about you, my dear."

Rhian found the demand difficult to execute. Her own childhood, debut, and business concerns had to be glossed over. In the retelling, she sounded a very dull sort of person, and she was afraid Lady Margaret saw through her guise.

"So you have simply lived here with your father for the past six years?"

"Yes," she replied.

"And your sister? Do you see her very often?"

Rhian looked at Lady Margaret in surprise. She had certainly done her homework. It would do no good, Rhian guessed, to deny Penelope's existence, so she plunged in head first.

"I don't see very much of my sister. She married an Irish banker and retired from the ton. She has one child, a son, who will inherit my father's title and lands, such as they are."

"I see. But your grandfather left this house to you?"

"You are singularly well-informed, my lady," said Rhian, unable to keep her irritation from showing.

"Where my son is concerned, I am. You may consider my questions prying, but I assure you, when your son is going to wed someone out of the ordinary, you, too, will make it a point to find out everything you can about her."

"Perhaps," said Rhian doubtfully.

"Mark my words. Especially if you and Jonathan have only one child. It makes a mother even more protective, even more overbearing," she added, her intimate smile making Rhian feel much more at ease.

"Well, Mother, have you finished interrogating my betrothed?" asked Jonathan as he entered the room.

"You're early." she said plaintively.

"Only a few minutes. Besides, if you want me to escort you to Aunt Lucinda's, we must be going."

"Oh, very well, but I'll be back a few days before the wedding, and we can have a long, comfortable coze then," said Lady Margaret, rising and presenting her cheek for Rhian to kiss.

"Then you're not staying in town?"

"No, I hate London. I wouldn't have come at all except my sister is ill—or so she keeps writing me—and I decided to spend a few weeks with her to cheer her up. She lives in Chigwell."

"I'm very glad I had the opportunity to meet you," said Rhian.

"And I, you, my dear. I think you're absolutely perfect for Jonathan. Welcome to the family," said Lady Margaret, taking her son's arm and heading for the door.

"Thank you. Good-bye."

"I'll be back tomorrow, Rhian," said Jonathan, grinning over his shoulder at her and winking.

The invitations continued to roll in; Rhian was amazed at the extent of her popularity now that she was betrothed to a viscount. They were destined for another ball, this one a masquerade, the type of entertainment Rhian had always relished for the number of *on-dits* she could gather for her column. But tonight, she would be among the feted, not a mere observer.

For her costume she chose a rich gown of emerald green with finest gold lace at the neck and hem; she felt like she could be the belle of the ball. Her mirror told her there were hundreds of women more beautiful, but one look into Jonathan's dark eyes told her otherwise.

Just as she had at the Fitzhugh's ball, Rhian basked in the attention reserved for the darling of the ton, the reigning belle of the Season, even if only for a few hours. Her partners reserved the very best *on-dits* for their dances with her; her little witticisms were met with amused appreciation. In all, it was another successful evening.

Rhian, always thinking of her newspaper, found it impossible to merely enjoy her success, and she committed to memory as many amusing anecdotes as she could to relate in the Quidnunc column. Only when she strolled in the gardens with Jonathan did thoughts of the newspaper disappear completely, his kisses effectively erasing any other thoughts.

When the time came to leave, Jonathan and Pockets escorted her home. Standing in the entrance hall, Rhian met her first disappointment of the evening. Jonathan was not going to kiss her with Tipton and Pockets looking on. He said a quick good night and lifted her hand to his lips.

"Good night," she said, frowning.

"Until tomorrow," he replied, reluctant to leave her, reading her thoughts as his own.

"Good night, my lady," called Pockets, standing on the top step.

"Good night, Mr. Sims."

Jonathan took a step out the door and Rhian called him back. "Jonathan!" she said, stepping closer, hoping he would defy propriety and kiss her.

Whispering, he said, "The garden in half an hour?"

Rhian nodded.

"Good night, my dear," said Jonathan for all the world to hear.

A light mist was beginning to fall as Jonathan slipped through the garden gate and into Rhian's embrace. Like a drowning man clinging to a buoy, he held her tight. Their lips met, and the world could have vanished without either of them knowing or caring. The mist changed to a drizzle.

Finally, Rhian shivered, whether from chill or from excitement, Jonathan didn't ask.

"We've got to get you inside," he whispered.

"The stables," said Rhian urgently. "The sleeping quarters are over the horses on the end closest to the house."

They dashed into the nearest doorway and out of the rain, choking on their laughter. The stall had been used for storage, and the floor was covered with mounds of fresh straw.

"Shh!" they whispered in unison, and dissolved into laughter once again.

When they had both recovered, Jonathan began removing his wet coat and then turned to help Rhian off with her cloak only to find she had changed to her night-rail.

She noticed his surprise and explained, "I didn't want Fanny to wait up for me."

Jonathan digested this and sat down on a pile of clean straw, asking, "Now, why did you want me to come back?"

Rhian ducked her head before revealing. "I was very good all evening in company, but I was really wishing everyone else to the devil so we could be alone."

Jonathan's low rumble of laughter told Rhian her confession was well received. Then he pulled her into his lap and began kissing her mouth, switching once in awhile to her eyes and ears. When he descended to her neck, Rhian gripped his head, moaning into his ear. Jonathan's tongue tickled the hollow at the base of her throat; his hand cupped her breast and he kissed the swell of white flesh. Rhian licked his ear, and he began to fumble with the ribbon securing the bodice of her nightgown.

Rhian felt a rush of cool air as he freed her breasts, but the sensation was lost in flames as he covered first one, then the other with feverish kisses. His hands replaced his lips which returned to delightfully torture her mouth.

His speech ragged, Jonathan breathed, "Should I stop?"

"No," whispered Rhian, moving so she was on top of him. Her gown riding up to her hips, Rhian began to move against him in the manner he had shown her, and Jonathan guided her steadily, the thin material of his knitted breeches stretching to accommodate his arousal.

"Wait," he said, moving her to one side so he could free himself of his clothing.

"No, Jonathan, now," moaned Rhian, not knowing what she was saying or what she was begging for, but frantic lest he should separate from her.

"Shh, I'm not going anywhere."

And he was true to his word. Having freed himself and her of all restraints, he entered her, covering her mouth with his when she would have called out. Quickly, the sounds she made changed to moans of pleasure as they moved as one, slowly, then faster, until both cried out in fulfillment.

Jonathan was the first to move as he pulled her nightgown down to cover her. At this slight movement, Rhian shivered, a last remnant of sensual pleasure overtaking her.

"I love you," he whispered into her ear.

"And I love you," she responded, kissing his bare chest sleepily.

He helped her sit up and began picking straw out of her hair by the moonlight. Rhian watched with interest as he replaced his clothing, knowing she was tired, but wishing he could stay with her until dawn.

"It's almost light," said Jonathan, looking out the door.

"Really?" said Rhian, gathering up the damp cloak and joining him. "I've got to go inside."

"I know. Kiss me now, and then I'll leave."

She complied readily and they parted reluctantly. Rhian hurried toward the house.

Part Three
Paradise Lost

Nine

Rhian wondered why the world hadn't changed. Here she was, waking up to the sounds of Fanny moving around the room, the quiet noise meant to wake her gently, she knew. She turned her head and saw the small tray with the cup of hot chocolate. The slant of the sun sent it streaming across the room. And there, there was the clock at the end of the hall chiming eight o'clock.

Rhian snuggled down in the bed clothes. The world around her may not have changed, but she had—a change so profound, she would never be the same.

"You did ask me to wake you at eight, my lady," said the maid, breaking into her reverie.

"Yes, Fanny, I remember. I'm getting up," said Rhian, yawning and stretching. "I've got to get to the paper before that broadsheet brings half of London down on poor Geoffrey."

"You shouldn't be going there at all anymore, my lady," grumbled her old servant.

"Nonsense! How else could the paper get published?"

"That Geoffrey—"

"Couldn't write the parts I do," said Rhian. Then she admitted grudgingly, "I suppose he could write the literary reviews; he and I discuss those, and he seems to have a good idea about books and such. But the Quidnunc? No one else could write that!" Rhian said proudly.

"Far be it for me t' tell my betters what they should or shouldn't do . . ." said the maid.

"But you will anyway," said Rhian with a laugh.

Fanny pursed her lips, closing the drawer she was straightening with a decided thump. Rhian sprang out of bed and went to put an arm around the maid's shoulders.

"I'm sorry, Fanny, dear. I'm just being a bear this morning, and you are giving voice to all my doubts about what to do with my paper once I am married. Forgive me?"

The maid patted the hand on her shoulder, saying, "It's not for me to forgive you, my lady. I just want you to be happy."

"And I am!" said Rhian, recalling the night before. But she didn't explain this to her maid, of course. Instead, she said, "Now, I must get ready. I'll wear the old black bombazine. That always keeps people at a distance."

Jonathan had never felt so light-hearted as he did making his way back to Pockets's house. He was not the only late night reveler making his way home in crumpled evening clothes, but he was undoubtedly in better shape than most of the bleary-eyed dandies he passed. He was drunk, but not with spirits, he thought, grinning foolishly at his poetic turn of mind.

That was what Rhian did to him, what she had always done to him from that first green-eyed smile she had bestowed on him.

He climbed the stairs and began to undress, removing his shoes and coat. He looked up and caught sight of his fatuous grin and shook his head. How many other men were lucky enough to marry such passionate women? And for love? He thought he must be the most fortunate man on earth.

Jonathan reached for the buttons of his waistcoat, and looked down, puzzled.

"Damn!" he said, realizing he must have forgotten it in the stables.

Hurriedly, he finished undressing, washed, and dressed again in buff-colored breeches, riding boots, and a bottle-green riding coat. He ran a brush through his dark hair and silently made his way to the stables. Here, he ordered his hack saddled and then set out for Rhian's house.

He wished he hadn't told her to lock the gate after him, but there was nothing for it, he would have to climb it. It wouldn't do to go through the front door, but he had to retrieve his coat. Her servants wouldn't gossip, he felt sure, but he couldn't bear to make her the talk below stairs, even among her own people.

Tethering his horse several houses down so he wouldn't bring suspicion to her doorstep, Jonathan strode down the alley quickly. Looking one way and then the other, he vaulted over the garden gate. Again he looked around cautiously before hurrying to the far stall and retrieving his waistcoat. One last look out the door, and he was back across the overgrown garden and over the gate.

Whistling, Jonathan strolled to his horse and mounted. Just then a hackney cab turned into the alley and pulled up outside Rhian's gate. Jonathan started forward to send the man on his way. Then he saw the driver descend, hold open the carriage door, and help a black-gowned female inside.

Jonathan's first thought, that one of the maids had been

called away, vanished as he caught a glimpse of a shapely ankle before the door was closed.

He sat there for a moment after the carriage pulled back into the street. Then, frowning, he kicked his horse and followed.

Jonathan came close to turning back several times, almost managing to convince himself that he had been mistaken. He was merely exhausted, having had no sleep and having had such an exhilarating night. But dogged determination prevailed.

He pulled back on the reins suddenly, causing his horse to paw the ground. He patted the glossy neck. "Easy, boy, let's just see what happens next."

The black-draped figure climbed down, waving to the driver before disappearing inside. Jonathan recognized the newspaper where he had placed the advertisement for Rhian.

"What the devil?" he muttered to his horse.

Enough, he thought, and started to descend. But then he heard another carriage and paused. It, too, stopped outside the office and a man stepped down and inside. Jonathan's blood began to boil.

But again, before he could dismount, another carriage arrived. This one produced another lady, dressed in lavender this time, but also heavily veiled.

Before long it was like a parade, one carriage arriving, disgorging its occupant, another coming to take its place. The occupants entered the office, staying for a few minutes and then departing.

Finally, the black figure he took to be Rhian appeared and entered the same hackney which had returned moments before. Jonathan again followed it, this time stopping by the entrance to the alley and ducking his head as she stepped down and hurried into the garden.

Jonathan's first instinct was to confront Rhian. But this idea he rejected. How could he confront her without admitting he had been following her all morning? Knowing how fiercely independent she was, she would never forgive him for such an intrusion.

Then he thought to return to the newspaper office. But that seemed silly, too. He was too tired to think straight, so he decided instead to simply go home and get some sleep, hoping some sensible solution would present itself when he was more rested.

Rhian slept the day away, satisfied that she had protected her newspaper as best she could from the onslaught of visitors. It had been worse than Geoffrey had predicted, people coming in person to respond to the broadsheet's advertisements moments after it reached its readers.

However their precautions had been sufficient to protect her own office and Townsend's printing domain from being penetrated. They had erected a solid wall dividing Geoffrey's office from the new reception area. It answered fairly well, allowing him to continue working unless he was summoned. Still, Rhian had offered to employ yet another clerk for a few days to help the new, shy Mr. Pilchard, an older man whose years of service had made him a bit too subservient to his betters. He had been intimidated by several of their visitors, and Geoffrey had been forced to deal with them.

But no one had ventured inside Geoffrey's area, much less broken through to her own office. Rhian hadn't liked going through their customers to reach the street, but it had been necessary. She knew no one could have seen through her veil, but she had been uncomfortable.

And what added to her discomfort, she realized, was the fact that she had yet to decide what to do about her precious newspaper. Intuitively, she knew without the Quidnunc column, the paper would lose the majority of its ton readers and would cease to exist. But how could she continue her business without Jonathan knowing? And what would he say if she told him?

The questions disturbed her sleep, and though the clock said it was time to rise, Rhian had to drag herself out of bed again. It was almost four o'clock, however, and Madame La Croix would be there any moment for the first fitting of her wedding gown. Aunt Rosie had also promised to come and lend her expertise and opinions for the occasion.

"That French woman and a helper are here," sniffed Fanny, coming in and pulling back the curtains.

"And Aunt Rosie?"

"No, my lady, Miss Fairchild is not here yet. I've put the dressmaker in the upstairs sitting room with the tea tray. Mr. Tipton said he'd see to it we weren't disturbed."

Rhian slipped into a wrapper, telling Fanny it made no sense to dress when she would only be taking it off again. She allowed Fanny to plait her long hair and tie a simple ribbon at the end.

Rhian paused, her hand on the knob. The sound of masculine laughter, mixed with low feminine giggles, drifted through the closed door.

"Oh, my lord, you're pleased to tease a poor Frenchwoman." said the seamstress as Rhian pushed open the door, standing in silence to observe the tableau before her.

The helper hovered in the corner, but Madame La Croix

was leaning toward her father, the bodice of her gown gaping open to show him her wares. Rhian cleared her throat, and Lord Ainsley jumped to his feet.

"Good afternoon, my child."

"Father," said Rhian.

"Well, I suppose you ladies have some sort of feminine things to take care of, and I know I certainly don't fit in," he said, bestowing a leer on the dressmaker.

Madame La Croix simpered, "That is a certainty, my lord. Not a handsome man like you." Then she looked at Rhian and became businesslike again. "We must make sure your daughter is the most beautiful bride London has ever seen."

"Rhian?" said Ainsley doubtfully. Then, seeming to recognize his faux pas, he bowed himself out, treating the dressmaker to a last leer.

"Your father, my lady, he has never remarried?"

"No," Rhian said coldly, turning with relief when she heard Aunt Rosie's voice.

"My dear girl, I'm so sorry I'm late. It was the most dreadful traffic I can ever remember," she said, nodding to madam.

"I'm just glad you are here," said Rhian.

"So am I! Now, where is the gown? Ah, there it is," said Aunt Rosie when the meek helper held it out for all to see. "Come on now, let's see how it looks on the bride."

Looking at her reflection in the cheval glass Fanny had brought in, Rhian had to admit that Madame La Croix had outdone herself this time. The gown was pure white with a train of satin and a flowing skirt with an overdress of the sheerest net Rhian had ever seen. On this, she had embroidered tiny pearls, so small as to be invisible, but they gave the gown an iridescent gleam. The bodice was in intricate lace, its neckline low and scalloped, accenting Rhian's slender curves. The sleeves, contrary to fashion's dictates, were long and fitted, pointing over the hand like a medieval maiden's gown.

The headdress was also net, a frothy confection embroidered with more of the seed pearls. It covered her hair and face, but was so sheer, her smile was easily detected.

Aunt Rosie clapped her hands after a few awe-struck moments. Then, after congratulating Madame La Croix, she said, "It needs to come in just a little around the waist."

"Here?" asked the seamstress.

"Yes, a little more. The wedding is taking place before the end of the Season and we don't want any gossip about Lady Rhian's condition."

Rhian turned scarlet, but the dressmaker only nodded her agreement. Promising a second fitting the following week, and a final fitting two days before the wedding, the dressmaker and her helper packed away the gown and their pins and tapes and left.

Rhian, relaxing in her wrapper, sipped the fresh, hot tea and listened in appreciation as Aunt Rosie began to tell her about the audacious broadsheet which had come her way that afternoon when she had called on Lady Easton.

"It is most diverting! I sent my footman out to find one when I came here. Some of the notices are obviously from the middle-classes, but there are a number from the gentry, or claiming to be of the gentry. For all I know, every one of them was made up just to sell papers," she added.

Rhian sat up, saying hastily, "I doubt that, Aunt Rosie. Any newspaper that did something like that—perpetrating a hoax—why, they couldn't stay in business very long. No, I'm sure the advertisements are quite authentic. Some people are simply that desperate, it seems," added Rhian, smiling secretly, remembering the advertisements Jonathan had used trying to find her.

"I do hope you're right; it makes it much more diverting to think they are real. The one that caught my eye was written by a lady of impeccable breeding, so she said, in which she said her prospective bridegroom had deceived her, leading her to believe he was a man of property. It said she wanted to find someone of substance to share her life and wealth. I couldn't help but wonder if it could have been Lady Holcomb."

Rhian permitted herself a laugh, knowing the perceptive Aunt Rosie had indeed guessed the author of that particular notice. But she couldn't allow herself to reveal the truth.

Rhian frowned at the thought. Once again she was forced to practice deceit, and with Aunt Rosie, of all people. She opened her mouth; she would tell the truth.

"Lord Pembroke has called, my lady," said Fanny.

"Oh, my, and I'm not even dressed!" exclaimed Rhian.

"Show him up. I'll entertain Jonathan while you go and change," said Aunt Rosie.

Jonathan couldn't prevent a grimace when he saw Aunt Rosie in the sitting room. So much for demanding the truth out of Rhian.

"My dear boy, how are you? You arrived at an opportune time. Fifteen minutes earlier and you would have been shown the door," teased Aunt Rosie.

"What?"

"Rhian was having a fitting," she said with an arch smile. "Of her wedding gown," she added.

"Oh, I see. Well, then it is a good thing, I suppose," he said, feeling gauche.

"Have you heard the latest?" she asked, anxious to tell her story again. When he shook his head, she said happily, "It is the most amusing thing!"

By the time Rhian entered the room, Jonathan had lost his grim outlook on life. Aunt Rosie's tale had explained everything to him, or so he thought. Rhian had to have been delivering a message for someone else, someone who didn't wish to be recognized. She certainly had no need of responding to the lovelorn advertisements!

"Good afternoon, my dear," he said, rising and kissing her cheek, his good spirits restored.

"Hello, Jonathan. I didn't know you were going to call."

"I was passing—"

"I'm glad," she said, blushing prettily as she took the seat by his side.

"If I hadn't, I was afraid I wouldn't have the opportunity to see you today. We hadn't made plans for this evening."

"I know. It's the first night in weeks we've had free."

Aunt Rosie yawned and rose. "And I, for one, am relieved. I plan to go home, put my feet up, and do absolutely nothing."

"Sounds like a splendid idea to me," said Jonathan, refraining from looking at Rhian for fear he would give away his own plans.

"And to me," responded Rhian.

"Good afternoon, children. I'll see you tomorrow, Rhian, for our shopping expedition. Are you coming, too, Jonathan?"

"Not this time, Aunt Rosie. I have some business to attend to before we leave on our wedding trip."

"Then I'll see you for Almack's." Aunt Rosie left the room.

After a few moments, Jonathan got up and strolled to the door, closing it quietly. He turned and made straight for Rhian, embracing her, burying his face in her hair. He couldn't reveal the hell he had been going through all day, but he wanted her nearness to wash away all the doubts he had suffered.

Their caresses and kisses flamed with passion, each recalling their intimacy of the night before. Jonathan's hands wandered over her breast, his strokes inflaming her longing. Her own hands moved against him, and he laid her back, covering her mouth with his before focusing his kisses on new prey. His hand sought to free her breast.

"My lady," said Fanny, knocking on the sitting room door. She waited a moment before entering.

Rhian and Jonathan looked up from their teacups. "I'm sorry, Fanny, did you want something?"

"Mr. Sims has called, my lady."

"Show him up," she began, but Jonathan interrupted.

"Show him into blue salon, Fanny. We'll come down there."

"Very good, my lord."

The maid left, and Rhian rounded on Jonathan, saying, "Why did you do that?"

"So that you, my sweet, impetuous nymph, would not be put in another compromising situation by your besotted betrothed."

She looked somewhat mollified, but she grumbled, "I don't see why. I'm not likely to do anything with Pockets here."

"True," he said, tickling her ear with his tongue before heading for the door. "But since we have no way of knowing how long Pockets will be here, I thought it best to safeguard against our hot-blooded natures. Less than three weeks now," he whispered.

As usual, Pockets was scribbling something when they entered the blue salon. He looked distracted and said, "Hallo, how are you doing this afternoon?"

"Fine, Pockets. Just as I was several hours ago when you spoke to me."

Pockets frowned. "I was speaking to Lady Rhian."

"I'm fine, thank you, Mr. Sims. Would you care for some refreshments?"

"What?" he said, putting away his notebook. "No, no, I only came to find Jonathan. I wanted to remind him he promised to attend a boxing exhibition in the morning."

"I hadn't forgotten," said Jonathan.

"Good," said Pockets, waiting.

"Was there something else?" asked Jonathan.

"Well, no, that is, I'd rather not say. Thought you might like to come along to the club with me. Don't wish to be rude, my lady, but, there it is . . ."

Rhian smiled at him and leaned over to kiss Jonathan on the cheek. "I think you better go."

Jonathan frowned at his friend who continued to stare at him like a puppy waiting for a bone. "I suppose I should. I don't think Rover here is going to leave without me. Good night, my dear."

"Good night, Jonathan. Good night, Mr. Sims."

When the two men were in the street, Jonathan turned and demanded, "What the devil was that all about?"

"I've got good news for you. I was talking to Aunt Rosie—"

"Aha! She sent you!"

"No, not exactly. Anyway, she told me the name of a company which might agree to publish your novel."

"And how does Aunt Rosie know about such things?" asked Jonathan, wishing he were still with Rhian.

"Aunt Rosie knows everything. Besides, that's not important. What is important is that I took your novel to them last week, and they've agreed to publish it. But you need to go there tomorrow and talk to them in person. They said they can't complete the printing until they do."

Jonathan just stood there, his mouth open, trying to digest what his friend was saying. He was torn between relief that someone had agreed to publish his work and fear that it would—or wouldn't—be well received.

"Well, will you go?"

"What?"

"I said, will you go? They're expecting you tomorrow at ten o'clock."

Jonathan grinned and took a step back up to Rhian's town house, but Pockets stopped him.

"Where are you going?"

"I wanted to tell Rhian."

"Tell Rhian? Have you forgotten what she said about novels?" asked Pockets.

Jonathan had forgotten, but he wasn't about to admit it. "Of course not," he bluffed. "But I don't see what that has to do with anything."

"She doesn't like novels and doesn't know why anyone would want to read one. Now, do you remember? Surely you don't want her to know you've penned a novel, especially before you know if anyone will like it or not. What if that editor who writes the literary reviews for the "London Report" tears it to pieces? You'd feel pretty foolish then!" finished Pockets knowingly.

By this time, Jonathan was nodding, agreeing. "Right," he said. "Not a word to anybody until we know if the thing is accepted or not," said Jonathan, turning toward their club.

"It will be," said Pockets, suddenly glum.

"Buck up, old man. Maybe everyone else has better taste than you do. You might just win this wager yet!"

Pockets shot Jonathan a disgruntled look and fell into step beside him.

Dressed in yet another elegant gown, Rhian went to Hatchards' the next day to select a few of the newest books for reviews. One of them, published by her sister's company, looked pretty dismal, and it was with misgivings that she chose it. But she couldn't shortchange her reading public, even for the sake of her sister.

Just as she settled in for a cozy read, Fanny informed her that her sister was below and wished to speak to her. Sighing, Rhian made her way downstairs.

Penelope looked up, an unpleasant sneer marring her features. "My, how elegant we are today."

"Good morning," said Rhian as cordially as she could. "Fanny tells me you wanted to see me."

"Yes, I do." But Penelope was not in a hurry and walked around Rhian, eyeing her gown with one raised brow. "So you are already in his keeping," she said finally with a wheezing snicker.

Rhian's eyes flashed dangerously, but she said nothing.

"I was just wondering, since I saw the notice of your betrothal."

"And you have come to wish me well," said Rhian dryly.

"Something like that. I was wondering who was going to stand up with you."

"Stand up . . . Why, I hadn't thought about it. I suppose Miss Fairchild will."

"Miss . . . I should have known you didn't have enough family feeling to ask your only sister!"

"You? Why on earth would you want to stand up with me? You can't abide being in the same city with me, much less the same room!"

"You could have asked!" accused Penelope.

"Very well, Penelope, will you stand up with me?" said Rhian in even tones.

"Not now!" exclaimed her sister. "I refuse to be second choice to some old spinster! Just let her do it! After all, two spinsters should be together!"

"Penelope!"

But her sister was already flouncing out the door. Gritting her teeth, Rhian went to the window and watched as Penelope climbed into her carriage. She would never, ever, understand her sister!

It was after five when Phillip Banyon called. He waited nervously by the fireplace for Rhian to make her appearance.

"Hello. Phillip. It's good to see you," said Rhian, indicating the chair opposite her own.

"Thank you for seeing me," he said, sitting on the edge of the chair.

"Would you like some tea?"

"No, thank you, I merely wanted to speak to you for a few minutes."

"Very well, I'm listening."

"I know you and Penelope don't get on very well, but I was wondering if you might ask her. . . . That is, I know she would consider it a great honor if you would ask her to stand up with you at your wedding," he said, finishing with a deep breath of relief.

"Phillip, I don't wish to distress you. You're the best of brothers-in-law, but I don't think that would be a good idea. As a matter of fact, I tried to ask her this afternoon . . ."

"I know. She came home crying."

Rhian was astounded to hear that her sister could care so much about her. "I didn't realize," she said.

"She doesn't like to let it show, but she feels it acutely that she no longer is accepted by Society. And the fact that you move about so freely, even though you are in trade also . . . Well, it is very difficult for her."

"I didn't know, Phillip. Of course I'll speak to her again. Don't worry. Perhaps we can come to an understanding."

"I hope so, Rhian. I do hope so," he said fervently.

Rhian jumped into the gig and laid the whip on Rabelais's haunches causing the old horse to lurch forward. Henry, sitting rigidly beside her, held on tightly, but he didn't say a word.

Tightlipped all the way home, Rhian threw the ribbons to her groom and jumped lightly to the ground. In the house once again, she tore off her hat and threw it on the bed, pausing to check that it wasn't damaged before she said loudly, "Blast!"

Silence greeted her outburst, and she recalled that she had given Fanny the morning off to visit her mother. Rhian looked around for something else to throw, but nothing unbreakable came into view, and she would never be so foolish as to break a piece of porcelain.

She sat down on the stool in front of the dressing table and drummed her heels on the floor.

Looking up, she caught sight of her reflection and grinned. Some things never changed. She had always thought such tantrums were the height of silliness, and they still were. But the smile had helped her regain her temper, and she stared at her frowning reflection without uttering any more blasphemies.

Her sister was without doubt the most aggravating person she had ever known. Going to her business, Rhian had been told once again, in no uncertain terms, that she was welcome to marry, but not with her sister's assistance. Rhian's own temper had flared, and they had ended once again with bitter words.

Next, Rhian had gone to the newspaper and tried to get some work done, but there were still too many people coming and going.

"They want another edition of the broadsheet," explained Geoffrey.

"That's impossible," she had said, giving such an idea short shrift. "We should never have done the first one!"

"Perhaps not, my lady. That Holcomb woman has been here every day and her questions are becoming very pointed."

Rhian frowned and rolled her eyes. "Do you think she suspects?"

"She thinks you've placed an advertisement in the broadsheet and keeps asking me why. I just pretend I don't know who she's talking about. But it is getting more and more difficult to keep my temper."

"I know," Rhian had said. "Being sensible is not always pleasant. But I appreciate your efforts, Geoffrey. And I assure you, there'll be no more broadsheets for the love-lorn," she added with feeling.

At least, Rhian told her reflection, that is one decision you have made about the newspaper.

Jonathan frowned as he pulled up his team outside the publishing house Pockets had told him about. Pulling away was a hackney exactly like the one he had seen that day in Rhian's alley. And getting inside this one had been another heavily veiled female.

"Must be my nerves," he muttered, handing the ribbons to his tiger.

"Getting leg-shackled kin do that to a body, guvner," said the groom knowingly.

"You must be right. I'll be back in a few minutes. Just walk them for me."

Jonathan entered the office, a Spartan set of rooms in-habited by a harried clerk who climbed off his stool, bow-ing and scraping as he showed him into the inner office.

Here, Jonathan was greeted by a round female who smiled at him like the cat who drank the cream. He looked around to see if her complacent expression was directed at someone else, but they were alone in the room.

"I am glad you could come to see me this morning, Mr. Brown," said the woman. "My name is Mrs. Banyon."

"How do you do," said Jonathan, shaking her hand.

"Your associate assured me you were agreeable to my terms, but I thought it best if we met face to face."

"Of course."

"Then you do agree to the terms? I know they may not seem very generous, but I assure you, if the book is suc-cessful, you will be well compensated."

"I'm not so interested in that," revealed Jonathan. "I just want to know what the reaction of the readers will be."

"Oh, I think it will be met very favorably, Mr. Brown," she said, accenting his alias and smiling complacently.

Jonathan thought privately that it was amazing how one red-haired lady could look so different from another. This one made him want to shrink away from her, where as Rhian . . . But he had missed something the dragon was saying.

"Pardon me? I didn't quite catch that."

"I said you can be sure I'll do everything I can to see to it the novel is well publicized."

"Good," said Jonathan, glancing toward the door.

"Then I'll say good-bye, Mr. Brown," she simpered.

"Good day, Mrs. Banyon," said Jonathan, moving with alacrity toward the door.

"You won't be disappointed, Mr. Brown," she said quietly as the door closed.

Ten

Rhian had loved Vauxhall Gardens since she was a child, when her mother had stubbornly insisted that she and Penelope be allowed to attend to see the fireworks display and the man-made waterfall. It had been linked for eternity to some little-girl dream of happiness and fairy-tale endings.

Now, the gardens had lost some of their exclusiveness, many of the ton complaining that anyone could visit them. But Rhian didn't care and jumped at the chance to go there with Jonathan, Aunt Rosie, and Pockets.

Aunt Rosie was less than enthusiastic. it being two days away from the engagement ball. She cautioned, "One of you will become ill from the night air, I know it!"

"Aunt Rosie, it's not like you to be such a Gloomy Gus," teased Jonathan.

"Oh, she's always been that way about the damp night air, Jonathan. Don't worry, Aunt Rosie. I promise I shall be the one who is taken ill so it won't ruin your betrothal ball," said Pockets. earning a haughty stare.

"Well! If you're going to talk nonsense!" she huffed.

"Leave her alone," said Rhian. "I understand your reticence, Aunt Rosie, but I do so love Vauxhall, and I haven't been there since my debut."

"Why ever not?" asked Jonathan.

"Well, how could she," snapped Aunt Rosie, "without an escort? Stands to reason, silly gudgeon."

All three young people stared in amazement, and the older lady explained grudgingly, "You must forgive me. I'm always like this just before I entertain."

"I knew we should have said no," said Rhian, concerned.

"Nonsense, my dear. I love to have people in, but I am a bit on edge before they get there. Now, enough of this old woman's complaints. Do we go by water or land?"

It was decided they would go by land, this being the best way to avoid a profusion of the deadly night air. All the same, Aunt Rosie wore a high-necked spencer over her gown and carried a muff to keep her hands warm.

Rhian wore a royal blue silk gown, cut low at the neck with a short train which she hooked over her arm. She wore the Pembroke sapphires around her neck, and a new matching bracelet Jonathan had had made for her.

He watched with admiration in his eyes as they entered the park, her eyes glowing with excitement.

"I would have brought you sooner had I known how much you like it," he whispered.

"It's like a fairy land," she responded, squeezing his arm and snuggling against him.

They strolled along the narrow paths to the waterfall with its man-made lightning and thunder, Rhian gazing raptly until Aunt Rosie declared she was tired and thirsty.

Aunt Rosie revived somewhat when they reached the Rotunda and were served thin-sliced ham and cold champagne. She became positively ebullient as she watched the parade of promenaders and dancers and pronounced judgment on each lady's gown and headdress.

"Now, that one on Lady Forbes is simply ridiculous. Why would anyone wear ostrich feathers coming out of a tiny sparrow's nest. And look! Now she is closer, I can tell it truly is a sparrow's nest. Only look, there are the eggs!"

Grinning, Pockets jotted this down in his notebook and said, "Now that's one that needs to be recorded for posterity."

"You don't really think those are eggs do you?" asked Rhian.

"No doubt about it," declared Aunt Rosie. "Last Christmas at her house party, she wore a crown of mistletoe and kissed every man there, guest and servant alike!"

"No!" said Rhian, watching the lady in question with a new eye.

"Don't look now, my dear, but there is your rascal of a father," said Aunt Rosie, covering her mouth with her fan.

Alarmed, Rhian stared at the dancers. Yes, it was definitely her father, and with him . . .

"Who's he dancing with?" asked Pockets innocently.

"My dressmaker," said Rhian coldly, watching as her father's hands began drifting where they shouldn't have. She stood up and left their box, mumbling something about withdrawing rooms.

Jonathan followed, catching up with her easily, and putting her hand on his arm. He nodded to a passersby and walked with her in silence until she felt able to speak.

"How could he? If he wants to . . . Why can't he be more discreet?"

"It's not important to him, I suppose," said Jonathan.

"No, it never has been. Even when my mother was ill, he and her lady's maid . . ."

"Not all men are like that, Rhian," said Jonathan, leading her down a dark pathway. He stopped, and Rhian could just make out his grin.

She couldn't resist teasing, "Is that why you've taken me here, to have your way with me?"

"Baggage," he whispered, covering her mouth with his lips, gently at first, and then more ardently. When he raised his head, Rhian held tightly, unwilling to let him go.

"We should be getting back," he whispered.

"I know," she responded, kissing him one last, lingering time.

"Do you want to leave?" he asked when they were nearing the Rotunda.

"Not yet," she said quickly. "We haven't seen the fireworks display yet!"

By the time they reached home, Rhian was asleep on Jonathan's shoulder. He woke her gently and helped her inside, kissing her brow before giving her a little push toward the stairs.

When Rhian had reached the landing, Jonathan turned to Tipton, saying, "When does his lordship usually rise in the morning?"

"That depends," said the butler.

"On what?" asked Jonathan.

"On whether or not his lordship ever comes home at night."

"I see. Well, Tipton, I would like for you to send me word the next time you see his lordship, sober and awake. I want a word or two with the man."

"Very good, my lord; I will not fail you," said Tipton,

outwardly a picture of servitude. But Jonathan saw the determination in the old man's eyes and nodded, satisfied.

Jonathan received the summons early the next morning, so he knew he was not going to find Lord Ainsley in the best of conditions.

Tipton opened the door himself and said solemnly, "Howard is serving his lordship coffee in the study, my lord. Right this way."

"Is his lordship sober?" asked Jonathan.

"As sober as I have seen him of late, my lord, if you'll pardon my opinion."

"I value your opinion, Tipton," Jonathan said simply, unwittingly earning the butler's respect and admiration.

"Lord Pembroke to see you, my lord."

"What?" mumbled his future father-in-law, shading his eyes with one shaking hand as he tried to lift the cup of coffee. The valet and butler left the room, and Jonathan poured himself a cup of the strong, hot brew.

"It's early for a social call," said the gravelly voiced Ainsley.

"Then don't think of this as a social call," said Jonathan. "It isn't, in fact. I want to talk to you about something that's been bothering me."

"Not wanting to call off the betrothal, are you?" asked the older man in alarm. "I'm afraid that wouldn't be advisable. It's all locked up, nice and legal. It would cost you a pretty penny to back out, Pembroke."

Jonathan calmed his trembling anger and sat down, leaning toward Ainsley until the fumes of the older man's breath and body filled his nostrils.

"I have no intention of backing out of the betrothal. I

take my obligation to Rhian very seriously. And speaking as her future husband, I want to warn you that you are in danger of losing your place of privilege in our lives."

Ainsley snorted derisively. "You wouldn't dare."

"Wouldn't I? Don't try me on this, Ainsley. We were at Vauxhall last night, and Rhian saw you wining and dining her dressmaker. For God's sake, man, have you no sense of propriety? First you bring your doxy here, into Rhian's home. But at least she had the comfort of knowing you were not flaunting her in front of the ton. But last night? You're not some young buck fresh on the town sowing your oats! Have you no pride?"

"I don't have to take this!" said Ainsley, rising unsteadily.

Jonathan pushed him back into the chair. "Let's get one thing straight. There are two weeks before our wedding. During that time, if you manage to behave yourself, I won't exact revenge. But one more episode to embarrass Rhian, and I'll have you thrown out of this house."

"You can't do that!"

Jonathan looked him in the eye and said evenly, "As Rhian's husband, I can do as I bloody well please with her property."

With this final volley, Jonathan stood up and walked out the door, leaving a very thoughtful Lord Ainsley in his wake.

The day of the engagement ball arrived, and Aunt Rosie was in a dither. She sent word to Rhian at noon that she required her assistance immediately. Rhian dressed hurriedly, but before she could leave, a second message arrived telling her she was not needed after all. A third summons arrived at five o'clock while Rhian was bathing.

"I am not going," she told Fanny. "If she really wants me there, she'll send another message."

"But, my lady, she is so old," said the maid.

"She is younger than I will ever be," declared Rhian. Just then there was another knock on the door.

"Another note, my lady."

"Read it," said Rhian, continuing to rinse.

"My dear Lady Rhian,

I am sorry to disturb you again, but the crisis is over, and I shall expect to see you at eight as planned.

R. Fairchild"

"See, I told you so. Now, hand me a towel, please. Thank you," she said, rising. "I knew Aunt Rosie was equal to it; she merely enjoys the dramatic."

"Come in by the fire," said Fanny. "You don't want to catch a chill," added the maid, who still felt if one was foolish enough to immerse completely in the bath, one was inviting health troubles.

Rhian spent the next two hours resting, as prescribed by Fanny, but she found it difficult. During her Seasons, her sister had been in charge of her come-out and had seen no need to go to the expense of giving a ball in her honor.

So, this was the first given just for her—and for Jonathan, she amended. If it weren't for him, for their betrothal, this Season would have gone very much like all the others.

She felt like Cinders, and a wicked smile curved her

lips. If she were Cinders, then she must have a wicked stepmother. There was no one else to fill that role except her sister Penelope. It was perfect casting, she thought gleefully. And tonight, she would go to the ball. But she didn't have to be home before midnight. She would waltz until dawn!

"My lady, my lady! Wake up! It's time to be dressing!"

Rhian came awake in an instant and looked at the clock. It was almost seven o'clock! She stripped off her wrapper and stepped into the petticoat Fanny was holding out.

"I'm going to be more like Cinders than I thought if I don't get moving," she said.

"Pardon me, my lady?" said Fanny.

Rhian laughed. "Never mind. Did you find my pearl earrings?"

"Oh, yes, my lady. They were in the drawer. But a box from Rundell and Bridges arrived while you were resting." Smiling, the maid stepped over to the dresser and handed her a long velvet box. "I think Lord Pembroke must have sent it."

Rhian's hands trembled as she opened the box. Inside was an emerald pendant, the large stone cut in a teardrop shape. Matching earrings and a bracelet completed the set.

"They're beautiful," said Rhian.

"Is there another note?" asked Fanny, her old eyes round and misty.

Rhian lifted Jonathan's calling card and turned it over. "For my beloved Green Eyes—Jonathan"

"Oh, my lady, he's such a dear man," breathed the maid.

Rhian smiled, pleased not only by the gift, but because Jonathan had remembered her gown was green. "Yes," she said, "a very dear man."

* * *

"I've a good mind to simply run away with you tonight my love," said Jonathan when they were seated in the carriage.

"It is tempting," said Rhian, pressing his hand. "But I'm afraid Aunt Rosie would never forgive us."

"You're probably right. Although earlier today, I think she would have thanked us."

"Did she send for you, too?" asked Rhian, laughing when Jonathan rolled his eyes.

"Yes, and I made the mistake of answering. By the time I arrived, she had it all sorted out and scolded me for jumping to conclusions."

"I know she's gone to a great deal of trouble—"

"Not to hear her tell it." He raised his voice to falsetto tones and mimicked, "It's the easiest thing in the world to throw a gala ball if one knows how, and I know how. And she has no idea why I was getting so frazzled."

"Poor Jonathan," sympathized Rhian. "Never you mind. I'll make you feel better." She kissed his lips, surprised when he did not respond beyond the simple peck. "Is anything wrong?" she asked anxiously.

Jonathan chuckled and shook his head. "You thought I was teasing, but I was dead serious. I've had about all of the waiting I can stand. I find I'm not a very patient man after all. If I were to kiss you the way I want to right now, we would never make it to the ball. That gown, the emeralds winking at me. Every time I look at you in the carriage light, I remember that first night when I fell in love with you. I'm ready to make you mine, my love."

"Two more weeks," she whispered.

The carriage came to a stop, and the groom opened the

door and let the steps down. Jonathan climbed down and reached back for Rhian, swinging her to the ground effortlessly.

"Now for the real challenge to my patience—being beside you all night long and not allowed to hold you in my arms," grumbled Jonathan.

"Not until after the ball, Prince Charming," said Rhian, receiving a quizzical look from him. "I have been feeling like Cinders all day, knowing the ball was being given in our honor, so I have cast you in the role of Prince Charming."

He laughed and said loudly enough for their hostess to overhear, "Let me guess, Aunt Rosie is the Fairy Godmother."

"Who else?" said Rhian.

"Who else, indeed?" said Aunt Rosie, presenting her cheek for each of them to kiss. "Clive and a few others have already arrived, but you are in time to form the receiving line," she said. "Rhian, you will stand beside me, and Jonathan, you will be on her other side."

"Yes, ma'am," he said saluting her.

"None of your nonsense either! And Lord Ainsley, you will stand on the other side of Jonathan," said Aunt Rosie, ignoring the astonishment her announcement produced.

"Papa?" said Rhian, wonderment in her voice.

"Of course, my dear," he replied bluffly, also ignoring her surprise and acting as if attending her betrothal ball, dead sober, was an everyday occurrence.

"Good evening, my lord," said Jonathan, masking his own surprise and bowing slightly to his future father-in-law. Their eyes met briefly with dawning understanding and respect.

"Son," said Lord Ainsley, extending his hand.

"Now, William, I want to make sure you understand when to present Rhian and Jonathan. I've scheduled the supper dance, a waltz, to be played at half past eleven so that, just before it begins, we will distribute champagne and you will go to the musician's platform. You will announce the betrothal and lead Rhian out in the waltz. A moment later, Jonathan will cut in and continue the dance with Rhian. After the music ends, we will go in to supper. Are there any questions?"

"Sounds like a capital plan!" said Ainsley, smiling at Aunt Rosie.

Jonathan and Rhian nodded their acquiescence and the two older people moved away.

"Did you notice how Papa looked at Aunt Rosie?" asked Rhian, wide-eyed.

"I'm not certain that is the real Lord Ainsley," said Jonathan.

Rhian laughed, saying, "I know. Why, he was so agreeable, and he wasn't even looking at her the way . . . You know, that way he has of looking at every female he encounters. And he is sober! Look! He's not even accepting any wine or port!" They watched as Ainsley waved the footman away.

"I think I could come to like your father," murmured Jonathan.

"So might I," replied Rhian, her eyes softening as she watched her parent engage Aunt Rosie in light badinage.

The guests began to arrive and the receiving line formed. While responding appropriately to the greetings and congratulations extended to her, Rhian managed to eavesdrop on her father's exchanges, finding herself relaxing with each conversation. She had never known him to put forth such an effort, especially on her behalf.

After an hour, Aunt Rosie dismissed Rhian and Jonathan, remaining "on duty" with Lord Ainsley for another thirty minutes.

Jonathan procured champagne for them before leading Rhian out for a country reel. Though the movements of the dance separated them frequently, Rhian enjoyed herself thoroughly, chatting easily with each gentleman she passed.

Their promenade after the music ended was punctuated by well-wishers stopping to greet them. Rhian forgot about wanting to be alone with Jonathan, enjoying the flattering attention.

"Happy?" asked Jonathan when they found themselves alone by the French doors.

"Completely," she said, bestowing an adoring smile on him.

"So am I, now," he responded, pulling her outside.

But their embrace was interrupted by Aunt Rosie who wagged a finger at them, saying, "I arranged this ball for the two of you, and I expect you to enjoy it."

"But we are," drawled Jonathan.

Aunt Rosie rapped his arm with her fan and said, "Not that sort of enjoyment. You'll have plenty of time for that after you are married. Now, come along. I'll brook no arguments from you."

She led the recalcitrant duo inside again, and assigned Pockets to dance with Rhian. Jonathan, she introduced to a young miss who was in her first Season and appeared to be more at home with the wall than with the dance floor. Seeing something of his shy fiancee in the child, Jonathan set himself to drawing her out, succeeding very well. When the dance ended, she had her choice of several partners who had witnessed her blossoming.

Like magnets, Rhian and Jonathan found each other and watched as another set was forming.

"That was very kind of you," Rhian said, sitting down on a sofa.

Jonathan's brow went up. "What do you mean?"

"You know what I mean. You must have been very witty to bring out that color in the shy Miss Sheridan's cheek."

"Oh, just an *on-dit* or two to put her at ease and give her something to converse about with other partners."

"Well, it was enough to interest several gentlemen in her. I call that kind."

"I'm feeling very benevolent today. It must be the company," he said, pressing her hand and causing Rhian to blush. "I've counted it, you know, the number of hours until we are wed."

"Really? How many is it?"

"I don't want to say. It sounds much better to say we have only twelve more days to wait," he teased, his thumb drawing a heart on her palm.

"Jonathan, stop that, or I shall be forced to do something outrageous," she hissed.

"I'm all atwitter to find out what," he replied, laughing. "What if I do this?" He turned so that his body shielded her from the other guests, and he lifted her hand, turning it and kissing her palm. Rhian shuddered as his tongue drew another heart. He finished with another kiss.

"I see what you mean," he said.

"What?" breathed Rhian, incapable of more.

"Your expression is shouting that what you really want is to be in my arms, alone, preferably far away from other human beings—like in a stable somewhere."

Rhian turned scarlet, but she leered at him, stared pointedly at his lap, and whispered audaciously, "And you, my lord, had best watch what you say, or my seduction will turn into yours."

"Touché, my minx," he replied, turning back to face the ballroom.

Rhian danced twice more with unexceptional partners. Then, the musicians gave a sort of fanfare, and everyone turned to the platform where Aunt Rosie and Lord Ainsley were standing.

"Lords, ladies, and gentlemen, if I may have your attention. Lord Ainsley has an announcement to make," said Aunt Rosie.

"Thank you, Miss Fairchild. The purpose of this ball which Miss Fairchild has so courteously provided is to announce the betrothal of my daughter, Lady Rhian Ainsley, to a fine young man, Jonathan Stirling, Lord Pembroke."

Rhian and Jonathan stepped onto the platform, and there was polite applause while the champagne was distributed.

Lord Ainsley raised his glass and said loudly, "To the bride and groom."

The toast was repeated and glasses raised. Lord Ainsley held out his arm which Rhian took on cue. They went down to the floor, pausing until the musicians struck up the waltz.

Rhian marveled at how light on his feet her father was. After two turns around the floor, he stopped in front of Jonathan and, bowing, relinquished her to her fiance. There was another buzz of approval, and everyone watched for a few more minutes before Lord Ainsley surprised Aunt Rosie and led her onto the floor, causing other couples to join them.

When the music ended, Jonathan led Rhian into the

buffet supper, a lavish affair which consisted of lobster, duck, and smoked ham with no fewer than two dozen side dishes. The centerpiece was a huge ice sculpture: a depiction of cupid pointing his bow at two hearts. It was secured over a massive silver bowl into which champagne flowed from several lesser bowls poised above it, forming a waterfall.

"Aunt Rosie, when she does entertain, doesn't spare any trouble," whispered Jonathan to Rhian.

"No wonder she has been at sixes and sevens!"

Others were also in awe of the spectacle, and Aunt Rosie basked in their adulation.

Lord Hampton, still smarting from the ridicule he had suffered at Aunt Rosie's hands at Almack's, commented on how ostentatious the centerpiece was, but his derision fell on deaf ears, except for those of Lady Holcomb.

Rhian shifted uncomfortably in her chair as she watched Lady Holcomb lean toward Hampton, covering her face with her fan. The fan dropped, and her ladyship and Lord Hampton stared at Rhian with narrowed eyes. Rhian turned to Jonathan and lost her worries in his eyes.

With supper over, Rhian and Jonathan danced again, their easy movements around the floor bringing knowing glances and comments about their suitability. But Rhian found little comfort in these favorable comments as less kind views surfaced, spread here and there by the busy Lord Hampton.

She wished she could hear what he was saying, but there was no way. Even if the entire assemblage heard his gossip, no one would dare repeat it to her. Nor to Jonathan came the one bright consideration.

It was nothing, she told herself, because Lady Holcomb knew nothing, and everyone would attribute her mali-

ciousness to sour grapes over her loss of Lord Ainsley.
But Lord Hampton's word might be more readily believed.
And, for the first time, Rhian wished with all her heart
she had made a clean breast of everything with Jonathan,
revealing her involvement with the newspaper—with
trade.

"Are you tired, my love?" he asked, gazing down with
concern at her strained countenance.

"A little," she admitted.

"Perhaps we should be going. I think it would all right.
Others have started to leave, too. And I do have to leave
town in the morning. I wish you could come to Silveroaks
with me, but that will have to wait."

"I wish I could come; I'm going to miss you," said
Rhian, her weariness showing in her voice.

"I'll be home before you know it. Now, my love, let's
get you home."

Jonathan was loath to let her go, but he insisted she go
straight up the stairs and into bed. He, however, was in
no mood for sleep. He considered going to his club, but
he didn't feel like being in company, either. All he really
wanted was to hold Rhian in his arms.

But he settled on the club, ordered a large brandy, and
drank it down without tasting it. No one dared approach
him, his face was so forbidding.

Finally, he left White's and walked back to Rhian's townhouse. He looked up and saw a light still on in what he
thought would be her room. He picked up a handful of
pebbles and looked up and down the street before pitching
them as hard as he could at the lighted window. He ducked
as he was rewarded by a shower of pebbles hitting his head.

When he looked up again, Rhian was standing at the window, smiling down at him. Jonathan made a motion for her to go around to the back of the house. Rhian nodded.

She unlatched the garden gate and Jonathan stepped inside, pulling her into his arms.

Rhian allowed herself the pleasure of his embrace for a moment before she whispered, "We shouldn't, Jonathan."

"Of course we should," he answered, "I can think of nothing else I would rather be doing. Can you?"

Rhian gazed at him, her resolution wavering. But love won out, and she threw herself into his arms. Jonathan picked her up and carried her to the stables where he made love to her, his movements measured to bring her unspeakable pleasure.

Rhian shuddered, curling up against him. Jonathan picked up his coat and covered her bare shoulders.

"I love you, Rhian. You have made my life complete," he confided before falling asleep.

Rhian touched his strong jaw and snuggled against him before she, too, gave in to her exhausted satiation.

Eleven

The coming of dawn brought with it a new day of business, and while Jonathan traveled out of London and Rhian slept through the morning and early afternoon, Penelope was hard at work. She sent out messengers laden with complimentary copies of the best novel of the year. With notes tucked inside identifying the author as a distinguished peer of the realm, a hero of Waterloo, and an active member of the London social life, the novels arrived at Hatchard's, Lord Hampton's, Lady Jersey's, and every other talebearer Penelope could think of.

The remainder of the novels, she sent to bookstores all over the city, offering extra copies to the owners if they were to sell out quickly. In the two largest newspapers Penelope placed advertisements meant to intrigue:

Lord P denies any allegations that the characters in his novel, *Tremayne's Tryst,* are based on living member of the ton.

The response was phenomenal. While Rhian slept, people all over London were sending out their servants to purchase this latest offering of Banyon Publishing. They scoured the pages, looking for themselves in the characters. Whether or not they identified anyone became less important by that evening when everyone was talking about *Tremayne's Tryst*.

The last copy Penelope sent arrived at Rhian's town house with the inflammatory message: "I chose this novel myself, and it will soon be all the rage. It was written by a powerful peer, and be forewarned, sister, it would be most unwise of you to malign this one!"

Rhian, settling in for a needed night at home, read the note, giving a most unladylike snort. "So the wicked stepsister thinks she can bamboozle Cinders! We'll just see about that," she said, picking up the book and opening it to the first page.

She finished it at five o'clock in the morning, her eyes bleary with lack of sleep. On the one hand, it had been a passable book, she reflected, but she was not about to be swayed by her sister's threats. She shouldn't have stayed up all night reading it, she thought. Undoubtedly, her discernment had been affected.

She flipped back to the opening pages and frowned. How could she take a book seriously with a hero named Herodotus Tremayne and a heroine called Artemis who was an expert with a bow and arrow? Obviously the author was some staid old scholar more enamored of Greek literature than producing a popular novel.

With this in mind, and her sister's barbed missive in front of her, Rhian sat down at her desk to write a scathing review.

Two days later, still in his dirt from his journey back from Silveroaks, Jonathan called at Rhian's town house. She was writing acknowledgments for wedding gifts and looked up thankfully when she heard his voice in the hall.

Flying to the mirror over the mantel, she smoothed her hair and turned to greet him with a smile. Jonathan stood just inside the doorway to the study, his eyes taking in every inch of her. Behind him, a smiling Tipton shut the door.

Rhian fell into his arms accepting his kisses with an eagerness she had not known she felt. Breathless, they clung to each other, tumbling awkwardly onto the sofa where they continued their greeting.

"I missed you so much," said Jonathan, smoothing her ruffled hair. "I refuse to go to Silveroaks again until you are with me. It has never seemed so big and empty."

Rhian smiled at this and said, "Good," her lips tickling his ear.

"Oooh," he growled, taking her face in his hands and redirecting her hungry caresses.

When they had gone as far as they dared, they settled back on the sofa, arms still entwined, and related each detail of their days apart.

"And are you promised somewhere for tonight?" asked Jonathan.

"Yes, at a musicale, but I will send my regrets. Aunt Rosie won't mind in the least, and I would much rather be here if you'll come to dine."

"I wouldn't miss it. Let me go home and change. I'll be back in two hours."

"I'll tell Cook," said Rhian.

Jonathan rose to leave, smiling down at her. "It's good to be home."

After he had left, Rhian stretched out on the sofa like a satisfied feline. She hadn't realized how important Jonathan really was to her. While he was away, she had functioned quite normally on the surface. But seeing him again, she knew now she had only been marking time until he came home.

She stood up and straightened her hair and gown. Looking at her reflection in the glass, she shook her head. She was no longer the independent lady she had once been. In her place was a lady completely dependent on Jonathan for her happiness. And she didn't care! she thought, smiling at herself. She had never been happier!

"Welcome home to the conquering hero!"

Jonathan looked around and then back at Pockets. "What the deuce are you on about now?"

"Haven't you read the reviews?" With a flourish, Pockets gave him a copy of *Tremayne's Tryst*.

"What re . . . You mean about the book? Where are they? Let me see!"

Pockets handed him two newspapers, saying, "Of course, I shan't like paying you the money, since I know the novel was much too well-written, but it's good to know the reading public has an eye for quality literature." He peered over Jonathan's shoulder and said, "I told you it was a damned good piece of work."

"I hate to burst your bubble, old man, but I don't know that I trust these papers."

"Well, you should hear what they're saying at the club and even Aunt Rosie has read part of it and says it's good."

"You didn't tell her I wrote it, did you?"

"Of course not!"

"What did that editor write about it in the London Report? You know, the one who isn't afraid to give his opinion, the one with whom I usually agree."

"I haven't read his yet. Wait a minute. I have it here

someplace. I've bought every newspaper in the city just to see if they have anything about your book. Ah, here it is. Let's see . . . It says . . ."

Pockets looked shocked, and Jonathan ripped the paper out of his hands.

After he had finished reading it, he folded it and placed it carefully on the table. Without another word, he climbed the stairs; Pockets followed cautiously.

He found Jonathan at his desk, writing out a bank draft.

"What's this?" he asked when Jonathan handed him the paper.

"I told myself I would accept the opinion of the editor of the London Report, and so I shall. Here are your winnings."

"Jonathan, I really don't think—"

"Pockets, take the damned check before I shove it down your throat." Pockets complied, and Jonathan said, "That's better. Now, I'm going to have a bath and then go to Rhian's for dinner. If you'll excuse me . . ."

As Jonathan soaked his weary muscles in the bath, he scanned his novel. He didn't need to read it word for word; he practically knew it by heart. As a matter of fact, he thought as he closed it, it contained his heart. And it was good, even if he did say so himself. Damned good.

He stepped out and dried himself. As he dressed, his indignation grew and so did his anger.

Who did this editor think he was? Had he even bothered to read *Tremayne's Tryst?*

Putting the finishing touches to his cravat, Jonathan decided he would go and visit this man who thought his novel was a "trite retelling of some Greek myth." He had a few things he wanted to ask the self-important editor!

"Where is your employer?" demanded Jonathan of the wide-eyed Mr. Pilchard.

"I . . . She's not here," he said, blanching and standing to one side.

Jonathan pushed past the clerk and entered Geoffrey's office, stating bluntly, "Where is the person who wrote this?"

Geoffrey stood his ground, blocking the way to Rhian's office, even though she was not present. He rapidly put two and two together and declared, "He's out of town."

"He? Your man out there said it was a woman. Which is it?"

"I'm sorry, my lord, I'm not allowed to discuss that."

Jonathan narrowed his eyes. So the clerk knew who he was. Then he said deliberately, "Not allowed, is it? Not willing more like. And as for him or her being out of town, I don't believe that for a minute." Jonathan handed Geoffrey a card, saying, "Give this to your editor at the soonest possible moment. Warn him—or her—that I'll be back and that I demand an audience."

"Very good, my lord."

Jonathan was running late, but he waited around until both clerks had left the building and it was dark. He started to follow the one who had obviously been left in charge, but his desire to see Rhian again won out, and he rode in the direction of her house instead.

Tipton showed him into the salon where Rhian and Lord Ainsley were waiting.

"Good evening, my lord," he said, silently wishing Ainsley to the devil.

"Hello, Pembroke. I was just telling Rhian how much I would miss her when you take her away. It has been the two of us for so long, I don't know how I shall manage without her."

"You'll be fine, Papa."

"Dinner is served, my lady," said Tipton.

The menu was not as extensive or elegant as the food at Aunt Rosie's ball, but it was good English fare. Cook had a way with roast beef and potatoes, and they finished with her strawberries and clotted cream which were beyond compare.

Their conversation ran the gamut from the weather to horse racing, a favorite topic of Ainsley's, and they spent two congenial hours at the table. Finally, Rhian stood up announcing her intention of leaving them to their port and cigars, but her father stayed her.

"I'm going to visit a friend who has been a little under the weather. We're going to have a few hands of piquet."

Neither Rhian nor Jonathan believed this, but they accepted his departure with smiles. When he had gone, Jonathan offered his arm to Rhian and led the way to the salon.

"We have the house to ourselves," she said with a saucy grin.

"Except for the servants," interjected Jonathan with maddening prudence.

"But they would—"

"Miss Fairchild and Mr. Sims, my lady," announced

Tipton, causing Rhian to groan and Jonathan to grin at her.

"Show them in," he said reasonably.

Aunt Rosie and Pockets were all agog with the talk about the latest novel to hit London. Jonathan and Pockets exchanged knowing looks, but they revealed nothing.

"Have you read it?" Pockets asked Rhian, his eyes on Jonathan.

"Why, yes, as a matter of fact I have," she said, frowning slightly.

"What did you think of it?" he pursued. "We would really like to know your opinion."

She looked at each of the three faces in turn, and a cold wave of dread washed over her. "It was well enough," she said quietly and intercepted a silent exchange between Pockets and Jonathan.

The color drained from her face, and the room started to spin as the truth dawned. She slipped to the floor, her eyes staring, unseeing, as Jonathan bent over her and lifted her into his arms.

Then all went black.

"It's just nerves, Jonathan," Aunt Rosie was saying. "She'll be fine. A few days of rest . . ."

"She's awake," said Pockets.

Rhian looked up at the four concerned faces and tried to smile. She was lying on her bed; she could tell that from the draperies. Fanny waved something vile under her nose and she coughed, trying to sit up.

"Lie still," commanded Jonathan.

She fell back and closed her eyes. When she opened them again, she said softly, "What happened?"

"You swooned, my love. And don't bother to tell me you don't swoon; I'll not believe you," teased Jonathan.

"I won't."

"What happened?" asked Aunt Rosie.

"I don't know," she lied. "I suppose I had too much wine at dinner. And I haven't been sleeping very well."

"There, you see, I told you so. She only needs a little rest. I suggest we all go away and leave her to her capable Fanny."

"Very well," said Jonathan, hanging back after Pockets and Aunt Rosie left the room. "I'll call on you tomorrow afternoon. I don't want you to leave this bed until then, understood?"

"Yes, my lord," she whispered, tears stinging her eyes.

He kissed her brow and left.

Rhian waited until she heard the carriages pulling away. Then she burst into noisy sobs.

In the early hours before dawn, Rhian closed Jonathan's novel, hugging it to her bosom, the tears flowed silently. No longer out to prove her superiority to her sister, she had noticed the polished style and appreciated the sumptuous imagery. She could easily identify the characters whose names had distracted her during that first critical reading. Jonathan's story was their story, from the first, complex meeting to the final consummation of their love. He had poured his whole heart into the telling of their courtship, and she . . .

Tears flowed anew.

Putting the volume aside, Rhian went to her desk and picked up her pen. A scant half an hour later, she sanded

the new review, folding it carefully. Then she pulled the
bell rope and asked Fanny to bring her hot water to bathe.

Dressed in her usual black gown and veil, Rhian drove
her gig out of the stable yard, Henry at her side. She had
not wanted to waste time sending for Possum and his
hackney cab, and she felt sure they would be safe at that
early hour of the morning.

They pulled up outside the newspaper office, and Rhian
handed the ribbons to Henry. "Tell Possum when he calls
for me that I want him to pick me up at noon."

"D' you think it's safe, my lady?" asked Henry uncer-
tainly.

"Yes. See? There is Geoffrey's office light. He's already
here for the day. Now, see you don't forget to tell Possum."

"I won't, my lady," said the groom with a nod, waiting
until she was inside the building before he turned the gig
toward home.

From the side street, Jonathan watched, speechless. He
started toward the newspaper, then stopped.

What was she doing there?

He watched as the lamps in the inner office were
lighted. A figure, decidedly feminine, hung up her hat and
coat.

Disbelief and denial was all he felt. Then the rage began
to wash over him, followed by humiliation.

She had known all along. She must have! The novel . . .
the advertisement . . . even their first meeting. She must
have arranged it all!

In a blind rage, Jonathan made his way back to Pockets's house. He threw open the door and stalked past the
startled footman going straight to the sideboard in the library. Pouring a tall glass of bourbon, he downed this
quickly. The liquid burned his throat and brought tears to

his eyes. With a nasty sneer, he poured another, nursing this one as a plot began to form.

Rhian frowned and looked at the clock again. Jonathan was late and that was unlike him. First there had been the note saying he would be unable to call that afternoon. And now he was late. Of course, she thought with a smile, he had never been too excited about attending one of Mrs. Bingley's literary salons.

"Miss Fairchild and Mr. Sims, my lady," said Tipton, showing them into the salon.

"Where is Jonathan?" she asked quickly.

"He said he would meet us there. Something about business in the city," said Pockets who had also been wondering about his friend's whereabouts. But he didn't mind escorting Rhian and his aunt to the literary salon. He wasn't reading anything, but he always enjoyed himself.

"Are you feeling better this evening," asked Aunt Rosie.

"Yes, I don't know what came over me last night."

"Too much excitement," said Pockets. "Shall we go?"

The carriage ride to Mrs. Bingley's passed without incident, and Rhian found herself feeling much better. She was happy to be going back to the place where she had first met Jonathan. From there, she would be able to start afresh, make a clean breast of everything. She would tell Jonathan about the newspaper, her sister's note which led to that awful and untruthful review, everything!

Jonathan was not present when they arrived, and Rhian watched the door from her seat in the back row, answering Aunt Rosie when spoken to, but not really attending.

As the second poet of the evening stood up, Jonathan

slipped into the chair by her side. He gave her a smile, but it failed to reach his eyes, and Rhian frowned.

This poet sat down, and Mrs. Bingley went to the front of the room, holding up her hands for quiet.

"We are most privileged tonight to hear a selection from one of our most recent publications. While one newspaper didn't do the work justice, the other reviews were understandably enthusiastic. Mr. Thornton has agreed to read it for the shy author who is in attendance tonight."

The buzz of excitement quieted, and Mr. Thornton, a middle-aged gentleman with a baritone voice began to read.

"Herodotus had always hated his name; it was not the name of a man of action, but he would not allow a slip of a girl to slight him or his name. He reached for her bow, intending to break it over his knee.

But before he could grasp the wood, the girl had pulled it taut and the point of an arrow was poised against his temple.

'I wouldn't,' she warned, pulling back on the string slightly. 'I am aptly named, and I'm not afraid to defend myself.'

'Nor am I,' he said, turning the table on her with a neat pivot so that the string was pressing on her lovely white neck. 'What is your name?' he asked.

'Artemis,' she breathed.

'The goddess of fertility,' he murmured . . ."

Rhian listened to the rich baritone, enthralled by his rendition of Jonathan's work. She closed her eyes, reveling in the repartee of the hero and heroine. Was that how

Jonathan saw their relationship? Was it as exciting as all that to him?

Everyone was applauding, and Rhian opened her eyes. Jonathan had left her side and was standing at the front shaking hands with Mr. Thornton.

Mrs. Bingley's high-pitched voice quieted the audience, and she said, "We are privileged, my lord, that you have chosen our little soirée in which to reveal your authorship. Such a delightful novel! You must be very pleased with its reception."

"Yes, it has been very gratifying," said Jonathan.

"There was only that one review . . . And who knows what sort of person wrote such slander. Or why, for that matter," she added.

Jonathan turned away from Mrs. Bingley and his eyes found Rhian. His voice clear and piercing, he asked, "Why don't we ask her why she felt it necessary to slander my work. Lady Rhian?"

A collective gasp rent the air. Rhian shook off the hand on her sleeve, ignoring Aunt Rosie's horrified exclamations. The sea of gleefully scandalized faces swam toward her, but she didn't swoon this time.

Rhian turned and fled, blindly seeking the ladies withdrawing room. She pushed past the surprised attendant and locked the door.

Jonathan elbowed his way through the astonished audience and followed. Pockets grabbed his arm and was roughly shaken off.

"Jonathan! What the deuce—"

"Shaddup!" he snarled.

"Lord Pembroke, please!" screamed Mrs. Bingley.

But he was not stopping for anyone. The hostess fainted,

and several followers paused to help her. Others stepped over her and continued after Jonathan.

"Where is she?" he demanded of the frightened maid.

She pointed toward the locked door. Jonathan's fist slammed against the wood, but there was no answer.

"Rhian! Open that door!" Still no answer. His voice quieter but more urgent, pleading, he repeated, "Open the door, Rhian!"

When there was still no response, Jonathan turned to the maid and snapped, "Where is the key?"

"It was in the door, my lord!" she shrieked.

"Then get another one," he ordered.

She scurried away, and Jonathan turned on the crowd of onlookers. "Clear out of here, all of you. Out, I said!"

Slowly, they skulked away, hovering in the hallway so they wouldn't miss any of the splendid drama.

The maid returned with the key, and Jonathan, nervous all of a sudden, fumbled with the lock. When it opened, the hinges squeaked ominously. The room was empty, the only movement a heavy velvet curtain swaying against the raised window.

Part Four
Paradise Regained

Twelve

Jonathan buried his head in his hands. He had missed her. How she had gotten away so quickly, he had no idea, but she had slipped through his fingers. Her servants denied any knowledge of her whereabouts.

He looked at the glass of brandy Pockets had poured out for him, but he didn't touch it. It might make him forget, and he didn't want to forget the sight of Rhian's stricken face when he turned on her. His soul deserved to be tortured forever by that image.

"I thought you might like to see this," said Pockets, placing a newspaper under his nose. "Not like to see it, but should see it."

Jonathan picked it up, recognizing instantly the London Report. In the literary reviews, the headline jumped out at him.

"TREMAYNE'S TRYST REMINISCENT OF MISS AUSTEN"

What followed was a glowing review with apologies for the first one which, it said, had been a result of indigestion and bad temper.

Jonathan moaned again. "She must have written this before she went to Mrs. Bingley's. It must have been typeset early yesterday. I'm a damned fool."

"True, but you know, Jonathan, all is not lost. And it isn't like you to give up so easily," said Pockets.

"Not at all," agreed Aunt Rosie.

"Leave me alone," he said, rising and walking toward the door.

"I never thought I could be so ashamed of you," said Aunt Rosie in her best governess voice.

"Not half as ashamed as I am myself," answered Jonathan, turning to go.

"Not for what you've done, Jonathan! For what you haven't done!" exclaimed Aunt Rosie impatiently.

Jonathan paused at this and looked at her, his expression not hopeful, only curious.

"All you did was ask her butler if she was home. You haven't even questioned her father, or her sister."

"Sister? I don't think her sister even lives around here."

"Nonsense, of course she does. She is married to a banker in the city."

"How did you know . . . Never mind. I'll go round and ask Ainsley her location."

"Good, and don't give up, my dear boy. I'm sure Rhiar will forgive you."

Jonathan looked surprised and opened his mouth to correct Aunt Rosie. Then he thought better of it. He had been speaking a great deal too much lately.

Lord Ainsley was out when Jonathan called, but he requested an audience with the servants. Tipton was reluctant, but his old heart was torn as he looked into the viscount's tortured eyes, and he agreed.

Jonathan asked them all to be seated, but he remained standing, actually pacing back and forth. The servants, down to Henry the groom, were assembled in the salon, perched nervously on the edges of their chairs.

"I would like for all of you to think if Lady Rhian dropped any little hints about her destination. Did she mention anyone's name, perhaps a relative or an old friend?"

They appeared thoughtful, but no one essayed a response. Finally, Tipton said, "I'm sorry, my lord. There are no relatives she could have gone to. Or friends, for that matter. She just slipped away, taking only one bandbox. Isn't that right, Fanny?"

"Yes, Mr. Tipton. I checked thoroughly and that was all that was missing. There was a little note. I didn't think too much about it. Miss Penelope was always sending my lady spiteful notes. I found this one in a novel Miss Penelope sent over the other day. Lady Rhian read it, twice, I think." Fanny handed over the note from Penelope, saying. "I am that worried about her, my lord."

"Could she have gone to her sister's?" asked Jonathan after a quick glance at Penelope's taunting missive.

"Ooh, I doubt that, my lord. They don't get along at all," said Tipton.

"You know," began Henry, stopping when all eyes turned on him.

"Go on, Henry, is it?" said Jonathan.

"She might have gotten Possum to take her someplace."

"Possum?"

"The hackney driver who used to take her to the . . . That is . . ."

"I know all about the newspaper, Henry. Where might I find this Possum person?"

Tipton took down the direction and handed it to Jonathan. "And her sister?"

Again Tipton wrote down the address and gave it to Jonathan.

The servants all stood up and Jonathan asked, "When do you expect Lord Ainsley?"

"He's been away from home for two days, my lord. He couldn't know anything about Lady Rhian's whereabouts."

"Very well, perhaps I'll find out something from this," he said, tapping the papers he held. "By the way, what is her sister's name?"

"Penelope, my lord. Penelope Banyon."

Jonathan staggered against the door frame. Was there no end to the tangle of deceit?

Jonathan waited in the formal drawing room for Rhian's sister to appear. When she did, he was not surprised to be facing his publisher.

"We meet again," he said dryly.

"Yes, indeed, my lord. Won't you be seated? I'll have Carruthers bring tea."

"Don't bother, Mrs. Banyon. I've come to ask if you have seen or had communications with Rhian since last night."

Penelope gave a falsetto laugh. "Oh, la, my lord, I am not my sister's keeper."

"I didn't ask you if you were, madam. She has disappeared, and I want to find her."

"Someone has abducted her?" asked Penelope, sounding concerned.

"No, she has run away, thanks to me."

"Then I don't believe I would tell you, my lord, even if I did know her whereabouts."

"Your familial loyalty does you credit," he responded sarcastically. "I read the note you wrote to her about my novel. No wonder she didn't look on it favorably."

"She never wrote good reviews of the books I published," snapped Penelope. "I'm sure she was just being honest."

"Really? Then you'll be interested to read her retraction that is in this morning's edition. Good day to you."

Finding Possum proved to be more difficult than Jonathan expected. He was not in the tavern Henry had indicated, or in his rented rooms. His wife just scratched her head and said he never told her anything about his work.

So, dejected and weary, Jonathan made his way back to Pockets's house. Here, he found a note from Rhian's sister.

"Pockets!" he roared after reading the brief message.

"Pockets! Where the devil are you?" he called, climbing the stairs two at a time.

"Here! What the deuce? Have you found her?"

"No, but look at this," said Jonathan, pulling shirts from the drawer and throwing them at his valet. "Pack a few of these, Pritchard. Make yourself useful."

"Very good, my lord," said the valet, folding the garments neatly.

"The Lake District? Why there? That's an awfully long distance to travel on a hunch," observed Pockets.

"It's worth a try, and it's all I've got. I remember Rhian mentioning spending the summer there when her mother was still alive. Now, look, while I'm gone, I want you to check with Tipton every day. If Rhian turns up at home, send me an express."

"You can count on me. Good luck," said Pockets, clasping Jonathan's hand.

"Thanks, I'll need it."

* * *

Three days on the road, a broken axle, impossible job horses, and a shredded temper brought Jonathan to Kendal in Westmorland. He asked after Rhian at the posting inn, but was told no one of her description was staying there. Turning away, he was halted by a barmaid in the taproom.

"Psst, my lord," she hissed.

"Yes?"

"You're looking for a lady with red hair?"

"That's right. Have you seen her?"

"I saw her when I was at my brother's place on the road to Windermere."

"When was that?"

"It's been two or three days. She came in on the mail and rented a gig and driver to take her on up to the lake."

"Where can I find your brother?" asked Jonathan, hardly able to contain his excitement. It might not be Rhian, but it was the nearest thing to hope he had allowed himself to feel since leaving London.

"Take the north road at the end of the village. You can't miss it. He's got a little tavern."

"Thank you, Miss," said Jonathan, pressing a gold sovereign into her palm.

The rough landlord Jonathan encountered at the tavern was more close-mouthed. Answering in monosyllables, he finally admitted there had been a red-haired lady who stopped by.

"And did you take her up to Windermere?"

"Couldn't say," replied the taciturn landlord.

Controlling his temper, Jonathan explained, "The lady I'm looking for is my wife. We had a quarrel and I merely want to find her so we can make up. Now, did you drive her up to Windermere?"

Still, the man remained silent until a feminine voice

declared, "Oh, tell 'im wot 'e wants t' know, Bagford. "E's not leavin' till ye do."

Bagford glared at his better half before saying grudgingly, "Yes, I took 'er up there. Left 'er at a cottage near one o' the smaller lakes."

"Can you take me there?" asked Jonathan, handing over another coin. When the man hesitated, he took out another and tossed it in the air, catching it handily.

"I'll take ye," said the landlord.

Jonathan knocked on the door, entering the cottage when no one answered. He walked back to the door and waved Bagford away. Going back inside, Jonathan began to search the bedroom for clues as to the occupant's identity. He had no trouble identifying Rhian's gowns. None of her new ones were there, the ones he had purchased, but he recognized her old ones.

He sat down in the tiny parlor to wait for her return. After half an hour, his patience had evaporated, and he decided to go and search for her.

There were only two tracks leading away from the cottage, and Jonathan chose one, thinking pessimistically that the way things had been going, he had probably chosen the wrong one. But this time, lady luck smiled on him as he came to the top of a small rise and looked down across a small valley, a picturesque lake nestled on the near side.

Jonathan made his way down the narrow track. He stopped when he drew close to the water and watched, mesmerized, as a barefoot Rhian waded along the edge of the water. She disappeared behind a small copse of trees, and Jonathan followed silently.

When he came out of the trees, he saw her lying in a

meadow of colorful wildflowers, her red hair fanning out, embellishing the riot of colors. She turned on her side, facing him, and he realized she was weeping.

Suddenly, she became aware of his presence and sat up, her green eyes wide with wonder.

"Jonathan," whispered the wind.

But it was Rhian's voice, and he covered the short distance between them in the blink of an eye, gathering her into his arms, burying his face in her fiery hair.

They spoke at once, somehow understanding the jumble of "I'm sorry"s and "forgive me"s.

Rhian confessed, "I own a newspaper, Jonathan. I should have told you, but I was afraid you—"

"I know. I don't care."

"And Jonathan, I loved your novel."

He nodded, saying, "I read your review, your *second* review. I should have told you I was writing it."

Their efforts at conversation ended with kisses and caresses that spoke volumes. It was almost dark before they made their way back to the cottage.

"What now, Jonathan?" asked Rhian, her head resting on his shoulder.

"It would be a shame to let this cozy little cottage go to waste," he said, his arms around her waist.

"There's a church in Kendal," she said tentatively.

"We could be married in the morning. I had planned a trip to Greece, but—"

"I'd rather stay here, Jonathan."

"Are you sure? It's not very exciting," he said.

"Then we'll have to make our own excitement," she replied, offering her lips for his kisses. He obliged, picking her up and carrying her into the bedroom.

Epilogue

The bright summer sun warmed the stones on the terrace as Jonathan paused in his writing to watch a dark-haired, green-eyed toddler get up from her game of making mud pies and amble toward him. He took out his handkerchief and wiped her hands before allowing her to climb onto his lap.

"Tell me the story again, Papa."

"Which one?" he asked, tucking an errant curl back into her ribbon.

"The one about the beautiful girl and her knight."

"Very well. Once upon a time, when the world was sunny every day of the year . . ."

"Your father has work to do, Diana. You must let him get back to his writing," said Rhian as she came up the steps, her arms full of colorful flowers.

"I am working," said Jonathan, tightening his embrace on the little girl.

Rhian laughed and complained, "Penelope will never be able to publish your novel if you don't quit changing it every time Diana asks for a new version. And Pockets wants to read it early so he can mention it in the Quidnunc Column."

"Devil take him," murmured Jonathan, his eyes roaming over Rhian and a wicked smile curving his lips.

224 *Donna Bell*

"Papa is working," said the little girl, climbing down and returning to her mud pies.

Rhian laid the flowers on the stone wall, and Jonathan pulled her into his lap. "There, now inspire me so I can think of lots more to write about."

"Not in front of Diana," giggled Rhian, bending her head and kissing his neck.

"Nonsense, she doesn't care," he whispered.

"No, but I do," said Rhian, trying for a severe tone. "Save your stories for Diana, Jonathan, and finish this one for me."

"Look! Papa, Mama, a caterpillow." She ran back to show them her find.

"Very interesting, my sweet," said Jonathan. "Shall see if we can find something to put him in?"

"Jonathan, you must finish." said Rhian.

Winking at his daughter and giving Rhian a squeeze, Jonathan said, "Diana, tell your Mama that there is no end to the story. She doesn't realize that our love story never ends; it just goes on and on."